PARIS for two

PHOEBE STONE

SCHOLASTIC INC.

ISBN 978-1-338-04510-9

10 9 8 7 6 5 4 3 2 16 17 18 19 20

Printed in the U.S.A. 40

First printing 2016

Book design by Mary Claire Cruz

For Rachel Griffiths

Prologue

In seventh grade, it was Windel Watson. I was beside myself over him. I was swept away. He seemed to be everywhere. He was in the halls at school. He was in the air I breathed. He was even in the clouds in the sky when I looked up.

"Doesn't that cloud look like Windel Watson at the piano!" I would say to my only friend, Ginger.

"No way. That cloud looks like someone playing the drums," she would assure me.

But unfortunately during that year, I bumbled the whole crush thing with Windel. It all turned into disaster and embarrassment and humiliation. I was only twelve years old and I was already hoping to spend the rest of my life on a desert island!

Then near the end of seventh grade I found out my family was leaving town. Moving away for a year, which was a very good thing. Best cure for a terrible crush is a lengthy trip across the ocean. I was hopeful until I found out *where* we were going.

"Oh, no, no, no," I said. "Not Paris! Not France! Please not Paris! I mean, going anywhere would be better, to the North Pole, to South America, even to the moon!" Because I knew Windel Watson was also going to Paris.

I was at school when I heard. I rushed to find Ginger. She's a kid fortune-teller. Her mom is teaching her. We went into the cafeteria and sat at a table. Ginger got out her crystal ball and peered into it. "Oh! Petunia Beanly," she said, "something wonderful is going to happen to you in Paris! I see three bouquets."

I looked up at the ceiling. My heart lifted.

Then Ginger paused. "I think. I mean, maybe." She blinked and smiled at me in a pale, quivering way. "Sorry, I guess I'm not sure. The crystal just went cloudy on me."

But it turned out Ginger seemed to have a quirky way with magic. Because there *were* three bouquets in Paris. And each one opened a door and brought with it a sparkle and a spell. And who was at the heart of it in the end? Well, that was the biggest surprise of all.

Chapter 1

I am standing in the hallway in our French building trying to figure out how to get the little cage elevator to come down from its perch and take me to the second floor, which is called the first floor in Paris. If you ask why, everything here will drive you crazy.

I look up and watch the tiny elevator sitting in the shaft above me even as I push the button repeatedly. Nothing seems to coax it down. There is a Frenchwoman behind me talking to Monsieur Le Bon Bon, whom we met yesterday. He has a green-and-orange parrot perched on his arm. The woman is cooing and talking to the parrot. Then she gestures toward me, frowning, and says, "*Les Américains*." Which I think means "the Americans."

"Hello, I mean, *bonjour*," I say to them. It's the only French word I know so I try to put a lot of feeling into it.

"*Bonjour*," says the woman and then she switches to English. "You are leaving soon, I hope? There has been a change of plans, perhaps?"

"No," I say. "My dad got a sabbatical and we're here for a whole year."

"Ah," she says, "a sabbatical. Let me guess. Is that a suitcase?"

"No. No. Well, it *does* sound like a suitcase. Like, *Here comes the bus, don't forget your sabbatical!* But actually, it's a free year to go wherever you want. And Dad chose here," I say and my shoulders slump. I can feel them drooping down.

"I see," says the woman. "Well, I am the concierge in this building. I keep track of what everyone does here. I mean, who comes and goes. And everything else." She looks at me with her fiery lavender eyes.

"Oh," I say, backing up. I suddenly decide to skip the tiny elevator and I leap up the stairs, two or three at a time. All the while below me, I hear Albert the parrot chirping and the concierge cooing at him in French and Monsieur Le Bon Bon sighing with delight.

I get to the large double doors to our apartment, throw them open, and march in with a French bread called a baguette over my shoulder, humming *"America! America! God shed his grace on thee!"* Because one good way to really appreciate your country is to leave it and go to an awful place called France.

I march down the hall to the dining room, where Mom is brushing my older sister Ava's long blond hair. Ava leans her head back and Mom says, "Oh, Ava, your hair has grown so much! It's almost below your waist. It's amazing."

"Mom, mine is getting pretty long too," I say, standing in the shadow of the doorway. The windows to the balcony are open and I can hear the French traffic on the rue Michel-Ange whooshing by. *Michel-Ange* means "Michael the angel." "Look, Mom! My braids go almost that far too." I swish my head and my two dark braids fly out around me.

Mom keeps brushing and brushing Ava's hair without looking up. "Ava, you are surely Rapunzel with this heavy, lovely weight. So like me when I was young. Speaking of which, you-know-who called again this morning. I wish he would leave us alone, don't you, Ava? The past is the past and I don't want to be reminded. Don't you agree?"

Ava's beautiful face twists up and she closes her eyes and clutches her hands, one into the other.

"Mom," I say again. "I think *my* hair has grown too."

Mom glances up at me. "That's nice," she says. Then she gives Ava a long hug. "Oh, Ava, don't you agree? It's so easy for him to just show up in Paris. He lives in London with his new family for goodness' sake."

Ava bites her lower lip.

"Mom, I bought a baguette for dinner," I say, jumping up and down a little bit like I used to do when I was younger. "I noticed a lot of people on the street nibbling on the tops of their baguettes. Nobody can wait till they get home. Every French person I passed had a baguette with a chewed top."

Mom keeps on hugging Ava. And I lean toward the sideboard. I look up into the mirror there and see myself reflected in the shadows. I look like a small, stupid elf with my long brown braids.

"Mom," I say again. "Shall I put the baguette in the kitchen?"

"Hot diggety dog!" Dad says, coming into the dining room wearing a little beret. It makes him look like a chubby American baby who is trying to look French. "We're going out to eat at the best café in Paris this evening! Get your shoes on, girls!" Dad is very excited to be in France. You should have seen him in the Tuileries Gardens yesterday. He was practically skipping.

"Hot diggety dog?" Ava says, beaming at Dad with her sleepy green eyes. She is drowsy from being brushed and brushed, like a golden horse. "You have read that ancient book too many times, Dad."

"You mean my favorite book, *Madame Bovary*?" says Dad. "The very one I am here to study? They didn't use phrases like 'hot dog!' in those days, Pumpkin."

"They might talk about French sausages, but not hot dogs, right, Dad?" I say.

"That's true, honey," says Dad.

"Oh, I mean, yeah, I knew that," says Ava, looking down at her hands.

"Angus," says Mom. "You're being critical of Ava." She draws Ava closer to her, their heads leaning together.

"No, no, sweetheart, not intended. Not at all," says Dad, putting his cuddly arms around Mom and Ava both. Now they are just a pile of draping arms all entwined, Ava at the center. When I look at Ava, all wrapped in a Mom and Dad sandwich, she sticks her tongue out at me.

For some unknown reason, I kind of feel like, I don't know, like something in my throat hurts and wants out at the same time. Like I could write a whole book about being a younger sister. *Page one: If an older sister sticks her tongue out at you, do not do the same. This gets you nowhere. Instead throw yourself down on the floor and pretend to be dead. Don't move or answer anyone until the ambulance arrives.*

Hmm, I tried that when I was younger but it didn't work.

At the café Dad wants to sit at the outdoor tables. He walks around and chooses one that has the best view of the Eiffel Tower. Finally a waiter appears, putting his cell phone in his pocket. Dad looks disappointed for a moment. He wants everything to be old-fashioned. Then he nods at the waiter with great cheer and gives our orders to him in French, but the waiter quickly translates everything to English.

"Just like Rick Steves says in his book. It's part of the French experience! The waiters in this café are full of themselves," says Dad, whispering to me and smiling with appreciation. Then he pats *Rick Steves' Paris,* which is sitting on the table with us.

Ava glares at me. Green fire.

When the waiter brings our food, Ava cringes at the glass of pink grenadine and milk that Dad wanted us both to try.

"Girls," says Dad, "from now on we're saying good-bye to the American hamburger."

"But there's a McDonald's next door and I can see a hamburger right now waving hello to me," Ava says.

"Come on, Ava, take a sip of the grenadine. Pet'll try it. *She'll* love it," says Dad. "And I bet she'll pick up the language here pretty fast too."

Ava looks down.

"Angus, you didn't even ask Ava about her plans to get a sewing machine," says Mom, patting Ava on the arm and nodding at her. "It's so resourceful, Angus, isn't it?"

"Wonderful, Pumpkin!" says Dad, kissing the top of Ava's head.

"Yes, right away I am going to be looking for a sewing machine, Dad," says Ava. She gives me a quick snooty look and then she opens her little purse and puts on pink sparkly lipstick. I am only allowed lip balm.

"Me too," I say. "I made the dress I'm wearing a couple of days ago. All by hand. The fabric is watered silk. Do you like it, Dad?"

"It's adorable," says Dad. "And the little collar! It just slays me."

"Watered silk? Please. Don't encourage her, Dad. She wears these things to school and then she doesn't have any friends and she wonders why," says Ava.

"I do too have friends. I have Ginger," I say.

And Ava starts laughing. It's a trill, Ava's laugh, melodic and charming. And it cuts through me like broken glass.

Page twenty-three: In cafés don't just sit there. Strike back! Use younger-sister annoying footwork. That is, go for the chair!

I begin knocking my foot against Ava's chair, all the while pretending to be nibbling on my croque monsieur (a French grilled cheese sandwich).

"Quit it," says Ava.

"What?" I say.

Dad's getting smoochy with Mom. They've both had a glass of Châteauneuf-du-Pape wine and Ava tosses the waiter a semi-smile. He starts moving in a circle around the table, like something caught on a fishing line.

But Ava looks away, studying my new watered silk dress with her terrible, beautiful frown. Her eyebrows are so blond you can't actually tell if she's frowning. And that makes me even more unsure. About everything.

"It's silk," I say. "Silk is hard to sew. It's slippery."

"Obviously it slipped away from you this time. That dress is ridiculous. Mom, don't you think so?" says Ava. Green fire leaping, stirred by the wind. Moving fire.

Mom has her head on Dad's shoulder. It's dark and warm out, with lantern lights hanging along the outdoor café. A bunch of French thugs on motorcycles just roared up and are leaving their bikes rumbling and they are clustering around, speaking French in a raucous, noisy way. They didn't describe anything like this in Rick Steves' guide, which is now in Dad's pocket next to his heart.

Dad leans back and takes in a deep, long breath. "Ah, Paris, such art, such history," he says, almost singing.

The motorcyclists at the curb are shouting *"Imbécile! Crétin!"* at one of their friends across the street. And a man gets out of his car and leaves it sitting in the middle of the road while he talks to someone at the café. The line of cars behind him waits patiently until finally they get fed up and a whole string of beeping French horns fill the air.

Just before the waiter clears away the last of our dishes, Ava looks at my dress again and then she sweeps her arm up and points to the moon that is hanging above us, huge and yellow, as if someone propped it up there in a tree just to give everything this soft, foreign glow. But as Ava turns, her arm knocks over the glass of pink milk. It goes splashing across the table and rolls into my lap, all over my new blue dress. Ava looks back at me, and the lantern light shimmers across her storybook face.

"Mom!" I scream. "Mom, it's cold. Ava knocked over the grenadine. It's cold, Mom."

"I did not," says Ava. "I did not do anything. You did it!"

"No, Ava, it was you!" I say, starting to cry.

"Let's not get tearful over this, girls. Accidents happen. It doesn't matter who did it," says Dad, squeezing my hand. Then he looks over at the Eiffel Tower, which is lit up against the dark sky and hovering above us, stunning us with its overwhelming presence. "Ah, look, girls," he says, stretching his arms out, as if to swim off into the night. "How can you quibble over a spilled glass? This is Paris. Here we are. This is it!"

"Mom," I say, looking over at her. "Mom!"

"Honey," Mom says, dabbing at my skirt with a napkin, "I told you silk is not the best thing to use when you sew. Especially if you're going to wear it every day. It's just so impractical. You don't listen to me about that."

The waiter hands me a wet towel and I scrub at my dress. He sloshes away the dishes and the spilled pink milk on the table, all the while beaming at Ava.

Dad decides to splurge and we take a taxi home, back to the rue Michel-Ange. Michael the angel. I can just see him, wings outstretched, hair blowing, floating over the grand buildings in the sixteenth district. And the whole way home, being tossed about in the zigzagging cab, Dad and the driver are babbling on in French. Dad is clearly in heaven, saying *"Mais bien sûr!"* as we ride across bridges lit up with nighttime joy, as we bump over cobblestone streets and under arches, passing glowing boats on the river Seine.

All the while, I am feeling that pushing, hurting feeling in my throat. I'll soak the spots on the skirt when I get home. Accidents happen. But my blue watered silk dress might be ruined. I thought I loved it. Now I'm not sure. Maybe I should have chosen something other than silk. Mom doesn't like silk. I watch Paris spin by in lights, changing like those patterns in a kaleidoscope, green fire, watery silk blue, sparkly pink. And there among the sparkles, Windel Watson seems to flicker in and out, reminding me of my other mistakes. I press my head against the window, feeling like nobody's ever going to love me or my dresses.

Chapter 2

Before I had a crush on Windel Watson, I was a normal younger sister, used to shadows, comfortable in the darkness. Alone. Like everybody else in my seventh grade, I just thought Windel was this moody boy child who seemed to live in some other world. We had all seen him show up for history class, too many papers and too many books in his arms. Unpopular, unorganized, unnoticed.

And then one day Ginger's mom was doing this New Age conference in the nearby shopping mall, reading palms and stuff. Ginger went along to hand out flyers in the booth. So I met up with her there and she took me into this large building across the plaza.

It turned out to be a piano practice building with all these little rooms down a long hallway. Each room had a piano. You could peer through the little window and see someone practicing. You could hear piano music drifting in the air.

In the last room we looked in and saw Windel Watson sitting at a piano. He was playing this beautiful piece of classical music. It sounded like rain blowing across a rolling green field. Seeing him there with the horn-rim glasses and the sad dark eyes, playing Chopin's rainy, romantic nocturnes with so much feeling made my head spin.

Dad says thousands of writers have used literally billions of words trying to describe "love" without success. But I could tell him it is easy to describe. That moment a little bird that had been sleeping for so long inside me turned over. It turned over and its cold, still feathers began to warm.

Until then I had known so little about Windel, only the way he wandered into history class, often late. Now everything was different. Maybe his name was part of it. It wasn't Wendel, the normal name; it was off by just a letter. It was Windel. It was his secret life. His never-before-seen confidence. His smoky, hidden moodiness. His obvious passion. And it was the music.

Chapter 3

When we get home from the café, the concierge is on the prowl. Her curly, short henna hair shines under the hall lamplight. "You have a nice evening? *Très agréable?* No wild French savage attack you on the street or bite you on the leg?"

"Oh *non non non oui oui*," says Dad, laughing, pulling up a leg of his jeans and showing his chubby calf. "No bites. All clear."

"Dad!" says Ava. "Please."

"Angus," says Mom, "you are embarrassing Ava. She's fourteen, honey. Be a little more sensitive." Mom is wearing a shawl to cover her right shoulder and the tattoo she doesn't like, which she got before she knew Dad. She takes the shawl and wraps Ava into it. Now Mom and Ava are rolled up together in a pale, delicate cobweb.

Dad looks baffled but cheerful. Then he smiles and hugs them and says, "You mean no one wants to see my chunky ankles?"

Behind the concierge in her apartment, her TV is playing loud and fast. It looks like maybe *American Idol* dubbed in French. The unpleasant faces of the judges seem that much meaner with French coming out of their mouths.

My dress is cold and wet and I look down at it, still feeling that pushing in my throat. So I leap up the stairs ahead of everyone and stand in the shadowy darkness outside the double doors to our apartment. I am kind of shivering.

"The little elf, she is already upstairs! With the sad face tonight, *n'est-ce pas*?" I hear the concierge say.

"My girls," says Dad, sighing. "And my wife is a painter. Did you know? *Une artiste!*"

"Oh, I am not, Angus," says Mom. "He's being so kind. I haven't painted in years."

"Buddy, no. While we're here, you're going to sit on the balcony and sketch, just like Matisse," says Dad.

"Angus, I wouldn't know where to start. But you didn't notice I made Ava a French braid around her head. Doesn't it look like a crown?" says Mom, her voice sounding proud and misty at the same time.

I stand here, waiting. It's spring in Paris but my feet are cold. Some of the pink milk splashed into my shoes. Finally, when everybody comes upstairs, I slip off into my room, which is small and narrow. I am actually beginning to wonder if perhaps it was once the maid's room.

I take the watered silk dress off and lay it on my bed, looking at the stains. Maybe I should just throw it away. I decide instead to take it to the bathroom, which is down a long hall far away from *la toilette*.

I turn on the cold water in the tub. This is a bit risky. The tub doesn't drain well after a bath. The water sits there for hours, reminding you in a sorrowful French way that all things take time. Dad says the French are very patient.

I float my dress into the water. And it slowly circles and turns with its ugly stains, as if stuck at the bottom of a well.

The feeling in my throat is causing me to bumble more than usual, I think, because when I go back to my room I kind of stumble and fall against the big dark armoire, which takes up much of my room. I hear a clunk and a piece of wood drops off the side.

It figures. It's always like that. When one thing goes wrong, everything starts collapsing. *Page twenty-five: The life of a younger sister is just a tower of dominoes ready to fall over.* I pick up the piece of wood and then I call out, "Dad? Mom?"

I lean into the hallway. Mom is coming out of the kitchen. She has just opened the back hall door and found a small group of bottled wines, delivered like milk waiting at the door. We have traded places with the Barbour family. They have wine delivered to their back door. Dad squeals with delight.

I look down at the piece of wood in my hand. What will the Barbour family think? I mean, because I broke a big piece off the side of their antique armoire. I hardly bumped it. I didn't mean to.

I am so sorry, Monsieur Barbour, I am thinking as I crawl into my crisp, heavy cotton sheets. I have hung up my wet silk dress in the window on the curtain rod with a towel under it. The lights from nighttime Paris pour through its watery silk body. I can clearly see the big pools of stains all over the skirt. My ruined dress.

Now my head hits the pillow and I fall away past the Eiffel Tower and float under the wings of Michael the angel and then I am almost drifting into sleep. But I still feel that pressing in my throat, that pushing feeling. I don't know what to call it. Whatever it is, it hurts, that's all I can say.

In the morning through my open window, I hear the nightingale that seems to live in the courtyard outside our windows. It sings a certain string of notes every morning, "da de da da da de." I sit up in bed at the open window, listening. Then I lean my head out and whistle a string of notes in response, a little different tune, hoping the nightingale will answer me as they do sometimes in fairy tales. And wow, it mimics the string of notes, the same as mine, whistling them in the same way. I whistle the string of notes again, and again the bird answers!

I rush out of my bedroom and I practically bump into Dad in the hallway.

"The nightingale answered me!" Dad calls out. "I sang to it from my balcony and I heard it answer. It sang the same notes."

I stop there, looking at my cheerful dad in his fluffy, white, terry-cloth bathrobe. We both just stand there for a moment. Then I say, "That must have been *me*, Dad. I answered you and then you answered me."

"Oh," says Dad, looking pleasantly confused, and then he reaches out and hugs me. "My little nightingale," he says. "This city has something otherworldly about it. Doesn't it? Just the courtyard full of trees is enough for me. Can you believe it?"

Now Ava walks into the hallway wearing her white satin slippers that Grandma Beanly gave her for Valentine's Day. She stares at Dad and me, a thousand dark birds flying out of her eyes.

I retreat into my room and look at the damage done to the armoire last night. I sit here listening to the real nightingale singing outside, such a beautiful song, as if telling me something in a language I can't quite understand.

I pick up the piece of wood and look down in horror at the newly exposed area on the side. My eyes focus on the spot and I move closer.

What? I see a small built-in drawer. A drawer? It must have been hidden behind the wood panel that I knocked off by mistake. "Mom?" I call out. "Dad?" But the Barbours' apartment is large and they don't answer me. All I can hear is the nightingale singing its repeated call.

I touch the handle of the little drawer and I look closer at it. The knob is carved in the shape of a bumblebee with tiny wings. I finally pull gently on the knob. It doesn't give way. And then I realize the little drawer is locked.

Chapter 4

"Oh, where is Ava?" says Mom when I emerge from my room, curious and somewhat shaken about the little locked drawer. Why is it locked? Why was it hidden behind the panel?

I look up at Mom, and my dress hanging in the moonlight at my window floats across my mind. *Mom, it didn't seem like an accident to me.*

"Ava? Where are you? Oh, Pet, look who I ran into downstairs on the street! Logan Stewart from Boston. We'll have to have your parents over for dinner, Logan," says Mom. "This is such a surprise!"

Mom moves aside and I am suddenly standing face-to-face with an astonishing red-haired boy. Age fourteen? Right here in *our* hallway, standing right next to the temperamental landline phone that rings when you bump into it by mistake and looks like it's been here since the beginning of time.

"Um, hi," I say, jolting backward a bit and pulling up my slouching kneesocks.

"How great that your family is in Paris, Logan," says Mom. "We just don't know anybody here yet. It's kind of lonely. I miss America, you know."

"Yeah, there's a bunch of Americans from Boston around. My mom knows them all. The Watsons, for one. But they're only here for a couple of months," says Logan. "But I mean there are others too."

"The Watsons?" I say, kind of falling against a wall tapestry of Marie Antoinette with soldiers surrounding her. "Um, you mean, like, um, Windel Watson? Those Watsons? Your mom knows *them*?"

"Yeah, the kid plays the piano, right?" says Logan.

"Uh, yes," I say, squeezing my eyes shut. It figures. *The life of a younger sister is just a tower of dominoes ready to...*

"I guess it was a big thing for them to find a hotel that had a piano so he could practice," says Logan. "Not every hotel has a piano, you know."

"Oh," I say.

"Yeah, and there are other Americans too. I mean, but the thing is, you really want to hang out with French people, not Americans. I mean, that's what we're here for, isn't it?" says Logan.

The problem with younger sisters is their knees shake, easily and often. Especially when names like Windel Watson are mentioned.

"He's in town already?" I say.

"Oh, I can't wait for you to meet Ava," says Mom. "She's just beautiful. She looks like me, the way I looked, you know, when I was young." Mom laughs and kind of glances in the mirror above the phone. A disappointed shadow drifts across her face. "Ava?" she calls out again.

I look down at the rug. Logan almost pats my arm. "Hey, Pet's pretty too," he says. Then he smiles at me with his numerous freckles and his rolled-up sleeves and his necktie-flying-in-the-wind kind of stance.

"Me?" I say, trying not to scratch my elbow or fall over and start crying because the boy I loved, Windel Watson, my beautiful piano-playing boy, is in Paris and he hates me. Because I pulled a major younger-sister blunder. No, many, many blunders. My knees are still shaking because of Windel.

"Ava?" Mom calls again. "Oh, this is such a big apartment! You can feel lost and lonely here and *very* American among all this French stuff."

"I like the Louis the Sixteenth chairs and the long French windows and all the balconies. This place is a classic," says Logan.

"Dad has to have everything old-fashioned. We aren't even allowed to use computers or cell phones here," I say, finally giving in and scratching my elbow.

Logan follows Mom into the salon, the French word for living room, and sits down in one of the little gold-painted chairs. He's been holding a long wrapped package and he sets it gently on the floor.

"Ava! There you are!" says Mom, her face lighting up like fourteen birthday candles, one for each of Ava's years. "Oh, honey. Look who's here! Logan Stewart!"

Ava emerges from behind the grand piano in the far corner and walks across the needlepoint rug like a graceful cat, with her long hair all golden and glowing around her.

Suddenly everything in the room shifts. The light changes. Logan lifts his head and his face brightens, as if someone has just thrown a handful of sequins into the air.

I stand here feeling small and alone with all these Windel memories knocking around inside me like a hundred pianos pounding. *So soon? In Paris already?*

Ava stops in the middle of the room on the large flowered rug, stepping on the stitched petals of a white lily. She just stands there. Where was she? Was she listening to everything we were saying?

"Oh, Logan, I remember you from Boston," says Ava. "I always wanted to ask you, were you named after the airport there?"

"No," says Logan, smiling. "I guess it's a popular name and there are thousands of kids named Logan out there. But you know what? Logan spelled backward is nagol."

"What does *nagol* mean?" says Ava, lifting her leafy-green eyes.

"Well, that's a secret that all the Logans of the world keep. We're the only ones who know what *nagol* means," Logan says. Every time he glances at Ava, he kind of seems to float up into the air, like a sailboat lifting away in the wind.

Ava smiles at him and says, "Ava spelled backward is Ava."

"Wow, like the word *wow*," says Logan, looking at Ava and floating, floating.

"Yeah. Like *wow*," says Ava.

"Pet spelled backward is *tep*," I say, suddenly sticking my head up like a prairie dog out of a hole. And then I wish I hadn't said anything because *tep* doesn't mean anything and it sounds stupid.

"Oh, and Pet had a crush on this boy with the weirdest name in the world: Windel," Ava says and she rolls her eyes.

I kind of collapse inside, thinking maybe I'll just tell Logan that Ava still carries around her stuffed blue dog when she's home and she still sleeps with it.

"Windel is not such a weird name," says Logan.

Then Mom says, "Pet, do you have something to do somewhere else maybe?"

"Yeah, like on another continent, perhaps?" says Ava, laughing.

Logan looks at me sadly as if he knows what I am feeling. "Ouch!" he says. "Hey, you know what? I brought something. Flowers. I mean, yeah, they were for my mom but . . . here. These are for you, little sweetie."

Ava turns to the window with a dark look on her Sleeping Beauty face.

"Flowers for me?" I say. "Seriously? Oh, thank you!!!" And I tear open the package and purple irises spring forth in a kind of celebration. In a blur Ginger comes into my mind. She whispers, *I see three bouquets.*

"Great bouquet!" says Ava. "But you don't want to give the flowers to *her.* She won't know what to do with them. She eats flowers."

"Ava! I do not!" I say, holding the bouquet in front of my face because I feel I might be blushing and I would like to hide that.

Then Mom says, "Oh, Logan, would you like some tea? Pet can bring in the tray for you and Ava. Two young people having tea in the salon in Paris! Oh my!"

"Mom!" says Ava with a little laugh.

"No, no, that would be great," says Logan, laughing too. Sequins and sunlight and sailboats floating, floating away.

"Can I have some tea too? I am dying of thirst," I say, doing the younger-sister hop. Up one, back two. Hop. Hop. Hop.

I look up at Mom and Ava. Mom has her arm linked with Ava's arm. They are frowning at me and I have this sinking feeling that France is a very small country and it seems to be getting smaller and smaller every minute.

I sort of back out of the salon. I go into my room and take down my dress from the window. It is dry now but the stains are still there. I slide into the corner next to my armoire with the crumpled dress in my lap. I sit there and stare at the little locked drawer. Then I stick the end of a barrette into the lock and rattle it. But nothing happens.

Chapter 5

"Albert!!! *Non! Non!*" I hear the voice of the concierge echoing in the hallway the next morning. Then I hear a tremendous racket outside our apartment door. Much shouting and whistling.

I open our doors and look out into the stairwell. I see a flash of purple and orange feathers. Monsieur Le Bon Bon's parrot has escaped!

"Albert! Albert! *Viens par ici!*" calls the concierge. She rushes up the stairs with Monsieur Le Bon Bon looking woeful and worried just behind her. Albert flies around in the stairwell and then soars through our open double doors and begins diving and dipping around our apartment. He flutters across the salon with his purple-and-green-and-orange wings fanning. I swerve as Albert flashes by me.

"Albert is very beautiful," I say, looking up at the ceiling, where he has paused momentarily on the chandelier in our salon.

"Albert!" the concierge calls out. "No, no, do not say that he is beautiful. He knows this. Le Bon Bon spoils him and perhaps I do too. You come here, Albert."

For some reason Monsieur Le Bon Bon reminds me of a Tintin character with his small tailored suit jacket and his wide eyes behind his glasses. He watches from a corner as the concierge flies around the salon now with an umbrella in her hand. She opens it and closes it so that the parrot finally leaves the chandelier and heads down the hall to my room.

"This umbrella usually works! He knows he is misbehaving but when he sees the umbrella he thinks perhaps we will take him out for a walk. He loves the rain. Ah," calls the concierge, running down the hall to my room. "*Voilà!* We have him now, *oui. Fermez la porte!* Close it, the door!"

And so I do. Then the concierge and Albert and I are all contained in my little room. Albert, with his dazzling purple, orange, and green feathers, is clinging to my bedpost. "*Viens ici, mon chéri*, hmm, *oui*," the concierge coos, moving closer to him. And soon enough she reaches out and clasps him gently. Now he is perching on her fingers. She cups her other hand around his back. "*Voilà*," she says, encircling Albert in her arms.

Then the concierge suddenly looks up at the armoire. Her face jolts. She takes a few steps back. She looks away and then her eyes return to its large dark doors.

"Oh, it can be fixed with glue," I say. "I mean, Dad isn't handy at all but . . ." And then I realize she can't see the little drawer from her angle.

"I didn't know the armoire was still here. I thought it was sold years ago," says the concierge, walking toward it and then backing up. "I never come up here and . . ." Her face turns to shadows and sadness.

“Wait . . . um. What do you mean?” I say in what sounds suddenly like an overeager American voice.

The concierge just backs away out of the room. Her face is strained as she looks toward the armoire. Suddenly she hurries away with Albert in her flowery possession.

Monsieur Le Bon Bon follows with a large golden cage swinging in his arms. Down the stairs and around they go, chattering on, Albert now singing and chirping among their fast French phrases.

I close the double doors. I go back to my room, and stare straight at the big, dark armoire, looking at it from every angle, wondering, wondering.

Chapter 6

I hear the nightingale trilling again as it gets toward evening on the rue Michel-Ange. The notes go up and down and in and out among the sound of wind and leaves. I go into the salon where Logan's irises stand in a vase on the piano. I pick the vase up and carry it into my room.

"What was all the racket earlier?" Ava says, stopping in my doorway. "And what did I miss? What happened with the armoire?"

"Oh, nothing, Ava," I say, scurrying over and standing in front of the little locked drawer so she can't see it. After the parrot was taken downstairs, I tried again to wiggle the drawer open for the longest time but it held fast. "Uh, the concierge was just admiring the armoire, that's all. Because it's so old."

"Oh, I see," says Ava. Now she comes strolling into my room. She crosses her arms and starts wandering around, looking at everything carefully like she's in a public museum. Ava doesn't really like museums, though, and she usually hurries through them and waits at the exit, tapping her foot impatiently. So maybe she won't stay long or notice that I am pressed in an odd way against my armoire.

Ava passes by my little table and picks up a jar of old buttons. "What's this?" she says.

"Oh, Dad gave those to me. He bought them at a flea market," I say.

"Why did he give *you* the buttons and not me?" she says. Her eyes, rain and fire. Now they flow like the Seine river toward the bouquet. She frowns. Suddenly she starts laughing. She covers her mouth but that laughter squeezes out anyway and goes zigzagging around the room.

"What, Ava?" I say. "What's so funny?"

"Oh, nothing," she says, "it's just the way you were standing there."

"What?" I say.

"With that bouquet next to you. It just made me remember how humorous you were, how you bumbled everything with that funny-looking boy you liked, the child prodigy," she says and then she covers her laughter again with her hand.

"Windel is *not* funny looking and he is *not* a child," I say, backing up closer to the armoire, still trying to hide the locked drawer with my skirt.

Ava puts her hand on her forehead and paces the room a little more. She picks up a drawing I did of the Eiffel Tower painted red.

"I painted that today. I did it that way because the lady at the bakery told me the Eiffel Tower was red when it was first built," I say, kind of jumping up and down again. Doing the younger-sister hop.

Page thirty-four: Younger sisters tend to bounce and jump around in the presence of the older sibling. This is done to avoid unpleasant confrontation. Keep moving.

"Hmm," says Ava and she tosses my picture back onto the table. She walks closer to me, stretching her neck around. "Why are you standing against the armoire like that?" she says.

"I'm not, Ava," I say, trying to smile. "I'm just staying out of your way. My room is not the Versailles Palace, like yours. That's all."

Suddenly Ava gets bored the way older sisters do and, out of the blue, she just leaves.

The good news is, I don't think she saw the little locked drawer. I mean, I found it and it's my secret. Not Ava's.

Chapter 7

I take a huge breath of relief when Ava leaves, but the air seems to have been sucked out of my room. Ava's perfume lingers over everything. I feel like I am choking.

I flop down on my bed and stare at the plaster molding along the edge of the ceiling. The bad news is Ava mentioned Windel Watson. Just the sound of his name! It flies through me like a startled bird. And all my mistakes!

I didn't really bumble anything with Windel at first, actually. I just went every day to hear him practice piano. I mean, it's true I never missed a day. But that wasn't my fault. It was as if I had sort of fallen under a spell. That's all.

Yes, the whole thing with Windel started off as a harmless spell. It was autumn in Boston. I liked to walk through the orange leaves on the way to the practice building. I felt music and sunlight in my heart. I had only wished to sit outside his door in secret and listen to him play the piano. He never knew I was there. And I wanted nothing more!

But once I ran into Windel by mistake in person on Halloween.

That night everybody who lives on my street in Boston sits on their steps and hands out candy. When the kids and their parents started pouring through, a small bull and a bigger bull and a grandpa dressed as a matador stopped in front of me. I was holding a tray of candy.

As the little bull reached for it, suddenly I noticed the bigger bull in the papier mâché horns was studying me in a curious way. I looked up at him and I realized in the dim glow of Halloween light that it was Windel Watson out with his little brother and his grandpa. I wasn't sure if Windel recognized me from history class. He didn't say hello or anything like that so I didn't either. Instead I just poured about half the tray of candy into the little brother's bag.

Then the grandpa shook his red cape in front of the little bull and the little bull charged at it, as a sort of performance for me, a kind of thank-you. All the while, Windel seemed to be watching me as if I were a documentary film about the discovery of human life on Mars.

Soon the three of them went off down the street. Two bulls and a matador. I don't know how they ended up in my neighborhood. Halloween is like that. Ginger's mom would chalk it up to "the falling glitter of coincidence." But for me, it was momentous, recognizing Windel in a string of pumpkin lights, his face in the darkness, a sparkle of notes, a trill of melody. An almost smile. Amazement. *You? Here?*

About a month later, just before Thanksgiving, Windel's grandpa died. When I went to the practice building Windel's room was empty for almost a week. Then at school I saw him from a distance. He was walking across the soccer field in the wind wearing his grandpa's big tweed overcoat. I wanted to rush out to him and say, "Oh, Windel, I am so sad about your grandpa." But I didn't dare. Ava could do something like that, but me, I haven't got that kind of confidence. Younger sisters are smaller and we always come in second. We just can't do certain things, like talk to a crazy, windblown, heartbroken, tweed-coated boy in the middle of a snowy field all alone under the sunshine.

Chapter 8

"Pet, your job this morning is to take the garbage downstairs to the bins in the courtyard," says Mom. She hands me a big bag. Dad is behind a French newspaper in the dining room with a large bowl of café au lait in front of him. His face pops up from behind the paper and he smiles. "Pet, you want to know the word for 'garbage' in French?"

"Um," I say.

"It's *les ordures*," says Dad with his usual cheer.

"You mean like *odor*, like *stinky*, *get away from me*, that kind of thing?"

"Uh-huh," says Dad.

"This is *your* job, Dad," I say. "Dads all across America right now are taking out the garbage while you are lounging with a café au lait."

"Dads all across America are snoring in bed right now because of the time difference, honey," Dad says, smiling supremely and waving me off in his Beanly manner.

I sigh, passing Ava in the hall. She is wearing this really cool French shift, which has these big cartoon eyes printed all over the fabric, tons of them staring at you and they glow in the dark. She bought it yesterday when we all went shopping at the Galeries Lafayette. I didn't find anything I liked. All the dresses seemed to pinch me under the arms, cutting off my circulation and my sense of self-worth.

"Pee-yew!" says Ava, backing away from me and the garbage bag.

My watered silk dress kind of hangs in the air between us. *That wasn't an accident, Ava.* I feel that pressing, sinking feeling. I suddenly decide to throw the dress away. I put the garbage bag down by the door.

"Yikes, Pet, don't come near me!" shouts Ava, scurrying away. "Pee-yew!"

I go into my room and stuff my ruined dress under my arm. Then I clump down the stairs with my smelly bag. I push out into the courtyard, heading for the garbage cans.

There is a rush of sunlight out here and a stand of those clipped French trees with speckled green bark that are everywhere in Paris. Dad says they're called plane trees. And under those trees is a little table, some chairs, and Madame la concierge and Monsieur Le Bon Bon are sitting there with Albert in his beautiful cage while a noisy little boy chases a ball around the courtyard.

I deposit the garbage in one of the cans and then I push the watered silk dress into the mash. I shove it.

I stuff it. I punch it down. I close the lid. Nobody likes my dresses. Not even me.

The concierge is waving me over. Now that I have helped her catch Albert, I guess I am no longer "*les Américains*."

"Petunia," she calls. "You are coming to meet Monsieur Le Bon Bon's nephew! He is like you, *un enfant*. He is learning English. Jean-Claude, *viens ici*! Jean-Claude! He is eight years old. You see, like a little brother, *oui*? You talk English with him. He needs to improve his grammar."

Jean-Claude runs around the courtyard, bouncing the ball higher and higher. "Jean-Claude, don't do this now. You come to meet Mademoiselle Petunia."

Jean-Claude is dressed in short pants and long kneesocks and a little jacket, possibly a school uniform. His cheeks are like pink French roses. The brown of his eyes soft like the water in the mossy pool at the Tuileries Gardens. I sit down at the table and the concierge says, "You need to run with the ball, like *un enfant*, a child! Go ahead. What were you throwing away just now?"

"Oh, nothing," I say.

"Nothing? I think I saw *something*. Something pretty. You and the older one are not always getting along?" she says.

That pressing feeling rushes up higher in my throat. How does the concierge know so much about me already?

"No, Ava and I are not getting along," I say in a quiet voice. I look over at the garbage cans sitting in the dark corner. The pressing feeling seems to put its arms around me tighter and tighter. I will *not* cry.

Monsieur Le Bon Bon is very silent but sympathetic. Perhaps he is mute, like a Tintin character, under some strange Chinese spell. He is wearing small wire-rimmed glasses and today a little bow tie.

"Your mama, *elle n'est pas contente*? Not happy?" says the concierge.

"Oh, she's fine," I say but then I think about Ava. The shadowy way she doesn't want to talk about her "other" father. You-know-who. Her biological dad. Mom doesn't like him. Ava used to go see him but Mom didn't want her to. So she stopped.

"Your mother paints. *C'est fantastique!*" the concierge says.

"Maybe," I say, looking at the beautiful parrot in the cage on the table tearing at a slice of orange. The sunlight disappears for a moment and then reappears, dropping through the leaves above. I hear the nightingale trilling high up in the trees.

"What does the nightingale look like?" I say. "I haven't seen it."

"It is a plain little bird. But it has a magnificent voice," says the concierge. *"Magnifique!"*

"Oh," I say.

"He is not colorful like Albert. We all have different gifts, you see," she says. "If we all had the same gift, it wouldn't be a gift at all, *n'est-ce pas*?"

"The nightingale has a gift," I say.

"Mais oui!" says the concierge.

I kind of slump against the back of my chair. The nightingale calls again. I suddenly think of the little locked drawer. I look up at the concierge and I say very softly and carefully, "Um, about the armoire in my room, um, has it been there a long time?"

The concierge puts her hand over her eyes, blocking the sunlight. She turns her head away from me and goes silent.

Jean-Claude is running past us and suddenly he stops before me. "You 'ave plaits," he says, tugging on one of my braids.

"No," I say. "Americans call them braids. I think English people call them plaits. You want to be English or American?"

Jean-Claude looks down at the stone floor of the courtyard. Then he looks back up at me. His face is beaming. "American!!! I want American!" he says and his little hand becomes a gun. "Bam, bam, bam," he goes, shooting everything in the courtyard to pieces. "Bam Bam Bam Bam!" Even Monsieur Le Bon Bon is shot full of holes but he doesn't seem to mind at all.

"*Ce n'est pas agréable*, Jean-Claude! It is not nice. You sit down," says the concierge. "Oh, he has misbehaved, you know. Like Albert! This one has taken Monsieur Le Bon Bon's Asterix books. He has broken into Le Bon Bon's cupboard, picking at the lock. The little one is a terror!"

The wind blows. The leaves whisper. The nightingale sings.

Hmmm, the little one is a terror. He breaks into cupboards. What about my locked drawer? I am thinking, *Hmmm, perhaps the little one can help me?* Perhaps? *Peut-être?*

Chapter 9

Autumn leaves and old flowers brushing into snow. Boston in early winter, Halloween and then Thanksgiving. I was there outside Windel's practice room every single day. But of course, I was always careful that he never saw me, although sometimes I had to dash into the broom closet. Once, it was necessary to hide in a stall in the bathroom and I fell off the back of a toilet, breaking the porcelain cover. But I was pretty sure no one heard the crash.

When Windel first returned, his music had a mournful note because of his grandpa, but soon it seemed to grow deeper and better. I had been perfectly content to listen in secret to Windel practicing the piano every winter afternoon. But one day Ginger said, "Pet, you're in a rut. You gotta meet Windel. You gotta talk to him."

"Talk to him?" I said. "Me?"

And so Ginger pulled some strings (she helps out in the office) and landed me a volunteer job at the coat check table for a performance given by Windel Watson at his little brother's school.

"Me?" I said to Ginger. "You want *me* to say hello and take Windel's coat?"

"Yup," said Ginger. "Piece of cake."

It was very close to Christmas then, a snowy evening, cookies, cider, and me standing at the table in the hall taking people's coats. I saw Windel coming toward me with his little brother leading him through the crowd. Windel was dressed in a tuxedo and red high-top sneakers. And this was probably the reason I didn't notice anything else. I mean, it was such a surprise! Just like his music. And then the way he took his little brother's hat off and handed it to me. I mean, when gruff-looking people are gentle, oh, it's just that much sweeter.

I took the hat and the coats. But I wish I would have taken more *notice*. I did remember the little one had a cute hood. But alas, I was flustered and didn't recall Windel's overcoat or anything later. I mean, Ginger says I must have been cooked, fried by the sight of the tuxedo and the little brother and the smell of cider and it was Christmas. I mean, these things encourage crushes. It wasn't my fault!!!

I sat in the deep darkness at the back of the auditorium, admiring Windel's rendition of "The First Noel." When the lights went on I quickly stumbled back to the coat check table and began distributing coats as kids appeared. Windel and his little brother were among the last to show up for their coats. I pawed through the remaining pile nervously. In panic, I looked up at Windel. Then Windel pawed through the pile and then we pawed through it together.

But alas, his coat was gone! And as we untangled the pile, a strand of my hair got wrapped around one of the cuff links on his sleeve. I couldn't move my head more than a few inches from his wrist or it hurt. It was his right hand so he couldn't do much to get the hair untangled, though he tried.

"It was a tweed coat," said Windel, looking at me sadly through his horn-rim glasses as I stood hunched over with my head against his wrist. "Brown with little flecks of gray all over it." I knew it had been his grandpa's coat and that made it so much worse. He seemed to wear only his grandpa's clothes now, and you could always spot Windel from miles away, the wavering, swaying kid with music scores under his arm, the one wearing his grandpa's baggy corduroy trousers.

Finally the custodian snipped my strands of hair with scissors and I stood up straight and said, "Possibly, um, somebody's father took your coat by mistake. You know fathers, they never know what their kids' coats look like," I said. I wasn't sure if Windel was mad or not. I mean, with the dark Chopin eyes and the way he looked at me over the top of his glasses. And the half a smile. And the tuxedo and the red sneakers. I think I mumbled something like, "Oh, Windel, I am so sorry."

His brother needed to get home so Windel helped him put on his little hooded jacket. Then Windel shrugged his shoulders and patted his brother on the back. There were no coats left. The snow outside had turned ferocious. Finally the janitor came out with a big roll of bubble wrap and offered it to Windel.

The last thing I saw of them that evening was Windel holding his little brother's hand and heading cheerfully out into the snow, wearing a funny-looking cape made of bubble wrap.

I was left at the coat check table, standing there just dying, watching the wind stirring up the snow in great funnels of whiteness.

Chapter 10

"Jean-Claude, *bonjour*!" I call down the stairwell. "Yoo-hoo! Are you down there?" We have just returned from a trip in a rented car to visit Flaubert's house outside of Paris. Dad loves Gustave Flaubert, the author of *Madame Bovary*. But we never got to Flaubert's house. There was a huge protest, a *manifestation* as they say here, which caused all the streets of Paris to be blocked.

"Désolé, mais la route est bloquée!" said the policeman standing in the middle of the street with his hand up to stop us. Dad seemed quiet on the way home. Now he walks into the apartment looking like a balloon that has just lost all its air, which is unusual for Dad. He's never down.

"Jean-Claude, I have something to ask you," I call again.

Jean-Claude comes racing up the stairs and into our apartment. He darts past me. Within moments, he has snagged Dad into a shoot-out in the salon. Dad is now crouching behind the piano with a ruler in his hand using it as a machine gun, firing at the sofa behind which Jean-Claude lurks.

Ava puts down her little suitcase, which she uses as a makeup carrier. Nobody even asked her why she was bringing *that* to Flaubert's house.

"Jean-Claude," I say. "Yoo-hoo! I need your help."

Jean-Claude rushes into the hall now and looks up at Ava. "Where is Logan?" he says. "I see you taking walks with him."

"What?" says Ava.

"Maybe," says Jean-Claude, "you fell into love of Logan."

"What?" says Ava again, stepping back a few paces.

"Ava," says Dad, breathing hard, brushing off his hands, recovering from the shoot-out. "You haven't had time to get to know Logan, so of course you don't love him. People mistake culture shock for love all the time, girls. Love and culture shock both make you feel charmed and stunned and lost. Ah, Ava, come on, give Paris her due. Don't misplace the glorious feeling!"

"Thanks a lot, Jean-Claude," says Ava. She frowns at Jean-Claude. He frowns back at her and suddenly I realize I have acquired, by accident, an ally.

"Well, what are you talking about, Angus?" says Mom. "Ava and Logan went to Notre-Dame Cathedral together yesterday. He read her a French poem in the garden there, for goodness' sake."

Ava blushes. Snow White with blond hair, Sleeping Beauty awake, the Princess and the Pea, rested. There is no telltale blushing in storybooks but I can see the red color climbing across Ava's face.

"He read her a poem?" I say. And oh, how I bumbled things with Windel.

"Mom, hush!" Ava whispers, crossing her arms and rolling her eyes over toward me.

I can hear water in the bathtub running. It sounds like it is about to overflow. Ava remembers it too suddenly and goes hurrying off down the long hall toward the bathroom, pulling her little makeup case on wheels. We won't see her now for a very long time. Yesterday Ava broke the world record for taking the longest bath in history.

"Jean-Claude, *s'il vous plaît?*" I say. "Please? Can you help me with a little something?" I walk to my room and wave to him.

Jean-Claude leaps forward in his kneesocks and short pants.

"My uncle thinks you will teach me more English," he says. "I am ready. I want to be Johnny Depp. Tonto! The Lone Ranger!"

"Come in and *fermez la porte*," I say. "Close the door, quick."

Jean-Claude slams the door. "I can kiss better than Logan," he says, leaning back against it. "Now is it time for an American embrace?"

"Jean-Claude, are you crazy? You're just a little kid. I am old enough to be your mama!"

"I like tall girls," he says.

"I am not tall. Ava's tall. I am a shrimp so far."

"Perhaps you will be tall soon," he says. "I like braids too."

"Jean-Claude, look, promise you won't tell anyone. This will be our secret."

"*Oooh là là*!" he says.

"Come here, can you help me unlock this little drawer?" I say, pulling a chair away from the armoire, exposing the drawer with its tiny bumblebee handle.

Jean-Claude sniffs at the air as if smelling the problem. Then he raises his little dark eyebrows.

"I need *un couteau . . .* for putting the butter on the bread," he says.

"You need butter?" I say.

"*Non non non. Le couteau* for cutting butter."

"Oh, a knife," I say. "A butter knife."

"*Oui, dans la cuisine!* In the kitchen," says Jean-Claude. He opens the door of my room and sticks his head out, reminding me for a moment of a smaller, more devious Tintin with his pen-and-ink stretching neck. Then Jean-Claude dashes into the hall.

"Jean-Claude," my dad calls out. "*Où est le* pistol? *Le* six-shooter!"

And then I hear a lot of bam bams and a bunch of pretend grenades exploding. I hear Jean-Claude's feet scampering down the hall and then too I see Dad scrambling after him.

Soon Jean-Claude returns and closes the door. He has a little butter knife sticking out of his jacket pocket.

"*Voilà!*" he says. "We slip this in, you see. It will open then, perhaps. Okie dokie?"

For some reason my heart skips and scampers then too. It flutters and buffets inside me and I stand here almost shaking. Perhaps there will be nothing inside the drawer. Nothing but disappointment. Emptiness. The usual younger-sister fare.

"Gold coins, perhaps?" says Jean-Claude. "You become *très riche*. You will take me in matrimony."

"Open it, Jean-Claude," I say.

And he shoves the butter knife along the top of the drawer and listens. We hear a little click and he pulls the drawer open. Jean-Claude glows with pride. He slaps his hands together and tilts his head. *"Voilà!"* he says again.

Inside the drawer there is a package wrapped in old flowered wrapping paper and tied with a ribbon. It is a gift. Clearly. An unopened gift. With a card under the ribbon. I was always taught not to open other people's presents. I mean, break a rule like that and Christmas would soon become chaos and disaster.

I look at Jean-Claude and he looks back at me. Then he reaches for the gift but I block him with my elbow and pick up the package myself.

It is light, almost weightless. I set it down on my desk and look at it. I twiddle my thumbs for a minute, mindlessly humming.

"It is a present for *me*," says Jean-Claude, rushing forward.

"No," I say, "it's a present for someone, but not for *you*. We shouldn't really be . . ." And then I leap toward it and grab it. I rip back the paper. It tears so easily.

Within the folds of tissue I see something amazing. Oh! I feel a series of crackles and splashes like sparklers lighting up one by one inside me. Oh!

There in my hands is a very tiny dress made of orange silk and maroon velvet. It has a silk bow at the back and a great orange silk sash. The dress is only about eleven inches tall. But so beautiful, all made with the tiniest of stitches. It is the loveliest doll dress I have ever seen. I am so surprised and so amazed that I start coughing.

"Une robe de poupée!" shouts Jean-Claude. "Not for me! Is too bad."

"Shhh! No, it's a doll dress," I say, whispering.

"Oui," says Jean-Claude, *"très ancienne."*

"Uh-huh, very old," I say, still kind of coughing and studying the doll dress and the card that is with it, written in swirling French handwriting. The only thing I can recognize on the card is a date, which I can't really read.

Jean-Claude shakes his head in a cheerful sad way when I look up at him. "I can't read that," he says, shrugging his little shoulders. "All I can read is Asterix."

"Since it was a gift for someone that we opened, we better keep this a secret. Okay?" I say. Then I push the wrapping paper and the card way to the back of the drawer.

"Ah, *oui*," Jean-Claude says, his eyes lit like little sparklers too. "I like to have a secret with *you*."

“Promise?” I say. “No telling?”

“*Mais oui*, I promise,” he whispers.

I stare at the little dress lying in my hands. I am astonished, dazzled, surprised, and very, very baffled.

And then one sentence pops into my mind: *Why was the dress hidden?*

Chapter 11

Last Valentine's Day, Ava got fourteen valentines. And she taped all of them around her mirror in the shape of a heart. Then she took a photograph of it and posted it online. I only wanted one valentine, not fourteen. Just one.

On Valentine's Day on the streets in Boston I always used to see college boys with bouquets wrapped in cellophane rushing past me. Everyone was carrying a bouquet that day, it seemed. And it was on one of those Valentine's Days that Ginger arranged my next encounter with Windel. Oh, but why did I go along with it?

Ginger knows all the volunteer stuff going on at our group of schools in Boston and she suggested *me* for the elementary school party on February 14. Windel would be there because of his little brother. I was to carry a bag of valentines from the first- and second-grade classrooms to the school gym where the party was to be held. And that wasn't easy for Ginger to arrange. The custodian was against it from the beginning because of the overcoat incident but Ginger managed it anyway.

And so I found myself on February 14 hauling a bag of valentines down to the elementary school gym. Windel was to be dressed in a mailman's suit and he was supposed to collect the bag from me at the gym door and distribute the valentines to all the little kids, the ones they had all made for one another.

Ginger smiled and handed me a pair of sunglasses. She said, "If you see the custodian, just put these on." Then she left.

For me it should have been an easy job. But being a second child, a low-ranking younger sister, I was nervous, shy, and even scared. If I had been Ava, perhaps I would have noticed that the big plastic bag had a long subtle broken seam down one side. Oh, I should have noticed! But alas, my lack of confidence encouraged my fear, which blurred my thoughts.

Well, at least I got to the gym door with the bag before it broke. And then, it split open and the entire contents spilled all over the floor. Hundreds of valentines were scattered everywhere in the hallway. And they were slippery too. I got so flustered that I skidded on a pile of them and my feet slid out from under me. When Windel opened the gym door in his mailman's suit, there was this girl (me) sprawled out on the floor in the midst of hundreds of kid valentines.

"Are you okay?" Windel said, looking down at me like his glasses weren't working, like maybe he needed a stronger pair to understand what was before him on the floor.

"Oh, Windel, I am so sorry," I said, getting to my knees, picking up a couple of wrinkled valentines and handing them up to him. Ginger hurried over. She had been outside and had missed the whole thing. She quickly began gathering up valentines for me.

But then something terrible happened. Ginger started giggling. And Ginger's giggling is *very* contagious. Unfortunately I was so stressed that I started giggling too and we both could not stop laughing. I laughed so hard I almost collapsed.

Windel leaned down and put one of his large piano hands on my shoulder and said, "Are you choking? Should I call the nurse?"

Some kids heard all the laughing and coughing and saw all the valentines and they came out to look and more kids followed. Soon everyone was running around, grabbing valentines and laughing and jumping up and down. One kid was zooming around wearing Windel's mailman hat, and there were valentines flying through the air.

Finally a teacher blew a big, loud whistle and the kids fell into a straight line and filed silently into the gym. Windel followed, looking back at me like a trip to the eye doctor was definitely on his must-do list.

On top of everything else, I left my favorite pink jacket in the hall there that day. I never saw it again. You might think that all this would have crushed my crush. But alas, it did not. No one seemed to have the talent or the secret passion that Windel had. I was the only one who had seen him practicing alone month after month, his hands flying over the piano keys. And one of those piano hands had been on my shoulder! And when he chased the kid who had stolen his mailman hat, he was giving another little kid a piggyback ride and that was so sweet.

Chapter 12

Today Ava is with Mom in the kitchen and she's crying. She misses Lucy, our dog, who is staying with the Barbours back in Boston. They are encamped around the kitchen table, draped together, inseparable. Dad is standing there with his hands dangling at his sides, looking sheepish and out of sorts.

"My sweet Ava," says Mom. "My firstborn child. We are so much alike, honey. I want to go home too. I have nothing to do all day."

"Buddy," says Dad. "I did a little shopping yesterday and guess what I bought for you? Some paints and a nice big canvas! Remember how you used to love to paint?"

"Oh, Angus," says Mom, "I wouldn't know where to begin. Honey? Why don't you take Ava to the Bois de Boulogne, the park where they have horse stables. Just the two of you, what do you say, Angus?"

"Fine, Buddy," says Dad, swinging his arms.

Ava looks sweetly up at Dad, reminding me for a second of the way it was when we were younger when we used to play together. Then, no one was as much fun as Ava. She could build wonderful houses of sticks and blocks. She brought in moss and flowers and rocks from the yard to make little beds and chairs and tables for our tiny dolls.

"Okay, I'm ready to go, Dad," says Ava, standing up. Today again she is wearing that shift with those cartoon eyes.

"I don't know if I would wear glowing eyes to the Bois de Boulogne," says Dad, adjusting his hidden money belt under his shirt, "but that's just me."

"Honey, if you wore glowing eyes *anywhere*, we might have to start marriage counseling," says Mom.

"Ha-ha, Mom," Ava says, putting her long arm over Dad's shoulder. She looks down at her shift and frowns. A slight dented look crosses her face. Then she glares at me and says, "Pet, that skirt you're wearing is not very French, actually."

"Actually, I'm not French," I say. And I pick up my backpack and sling it over my shoulder. *My* valentine's present from Grandma Beanly. Ava gets white satin slippers. I get a backpack. Go figure.

"Okay, we're off, then, Ava," Dad says, pulling open the double doors. He looks back at me. "Pet, honey, I hear you're going out to the Auteuil Market on your own today. Good for you, sweetheart! And guess what? When I was out yesterday I bought you this little pocket French dictionary so you can look up French words." He hands me a tiny red book. "It goes right in your backpack. The outdoor market is only a couple of blocks away. But be careful, okay?" he says and hugs me. My dad is cozy and warm and when he wraps his dad arms around me, I feel for a minute like I am back in America. Home.

"What did you get for Ava?" says Mom.

"Oh, Pumpkin, it wasn't like that," says Dad, looking befuddled. "The dictionary was just a spur-of-the-moment kind of thing. I'll get you one too."

Ava looks down at her dress again and gets all shadowy and slinks off to her room and shuts the door. "Pumpkin," calls Dad, "come on, sweetheart." He knocks on her door. Ava doesn't answer. Dad stands there and his cotton shirt suddenly looks wrinkled.

"Pet, move aside," says Mom, sweeping into Ava's room and closing the door.

"Mom?" I say. "Mom?"

We hear whispering and complaining. I hear my name and it falls through me, hot and white, burning like a comet.

Soon Ava emerges. She has changed her outfit. She's wearing bright red lipstick. She doesn't look my way. She just takes Dad's arm and pulls him out the door.

Chapter 13

I put on my purple jacket with puffy sleeves and covered buttons down the front that I sewed before we left "the States," as they call it here. Strange to think of home with its new name and from this new angle. The States. A wistful feeling pours through me.

In the hall Mom hands me a shopping basket and ten euros. "Honey, I need some fennel. Thanks for doing this," she says and then she shakes her head at me and adds, "Pet, you are the living limit. You should be wearing a T-shirt and jeans to the outdoor market. That purple jacket is just too . . ." She closes her eyes.

"What?" I say. "What, Mom?"

"Oh, never mind," she says. She blows me a kiss and waves.

I take the tiny cage elevator downstairs. As it drops, my heart drops too. Mom doesn't really like my purple jacket.

This elevator feels rickety and as if the wire could snap at any moment. But it doesn't. It always seems to hold. It is just like everything in Paris: delicate, old, balanced just right, and working mostly, in a French kind of way.

I get out onto the street and pass flowers in the window boxes blooming a French blue. The sky too is the same powdery forever blue. I pass a child holding a blue notebook sitting outside a flower shop on the corner. I nod and smile.

But then I walk by a poster in a round kiosk. The sight of it throws me backward off the curb as if in electric shock.

In horror, I look closer, hoping I am wrong. No. It's true. There's a picture of Windel Watson playing the piano on it. Large letters announce in English and in French: "Windel Watson plays Chopin in the Prodigies in Paris Series!" Windel's face seems to follow me down the street, accusing me, shunning me.

Feeling wounded, I cover my face for a minute. My luck. I thought I could leave my shame about the Windel incidents behind me, like a suitcase left on the shore. But many have tried and learned that leaving embarrassment and humiliation behind when you cross the ocean is never really possible.

Chapter 14

I bustle with everyone else into the open-air vegetable market, which is under tents at the Place Jean Lorrain. It is usually just a little leafy park in the middle of the intersection, but the area now has come to life, crowded with color and noise. I walk through tables piled with oranges and grapefruits and gleaming apples. Stands of flowers—peonies, irises, tulips, roses. I pass Frenchwomen with bags of vegetables bulging, leek tops poking out, spinach in bunches passing hands, artichokes, lemons, celery root.

If only spring hadn't come to Paris so beautifully just as we arrived from the darkest late winter back home. If only I didn't feel like crying one more time over Windel and his spectacular rise to greatness at thirteen years old. I look down at my jacket. It is too *what*? Mom didn't finish her sentence.

Then I go into an aisle of Indian bedspreads and skirts and scarves. Racks of saris blow in the wind and I get lost between layers of floating block-printed cotton, billowing blouses, and bedspreads. Did Mom mean too *purple*, maybe?

A group of African women, their heads wrapped in bright colored fabric, filter by me. A French mother rattles on to her small child and I can't understand a word of it. I don't understand anything. I am afloat in a foreign sea and I am tired of it. I want to go home.

Then the man at the flower stall says, *"Voilà, mademoiselle!"* He holds out a great big bouquet of tulips and I look at the color. I'm astonished. Some of the tulips are bright orange and some of the tulips are a deep maroon. And it sends another kind of sparkle through me and I can't believe my eyes. Ginger whispers to me again. Yes, *three bouquets.*

"Wow!" I say.

"Trois euros," he calls.

"Three euros?" I say. He nods. I count them out and hand them to him. And then the bouquet is mine.

The orange and dark red are the *same* colors exactly as the small beautiful doll dress back in my armoire. And that makes me laugh and hiccup. Suddenly I feel wonder and magic and I am flooded with an idea. Yes, I know exactly what I am going to do.

I still have twenty euros in my pocket, a present from Grandma Beanly before we got on the plane. Just beyond the Indian saris, there's a fabric stall and I stop there with my bouquet of tulips. *"Les fleurs sont jolies comme la jeune fille!"* says a lady selling fabric.

"What?" I say. "I don't speak French."

"Pretty!" she says, pointing to the flowers and then to me. I smile and begin looking through the piles of fabric. There, by chance I see a bolt of rusty orange silk, shining in the stack of yardage. Among the velvets, I also find a dark red. I hand the lady my twenty euros and she nods back at me and then at my flowers. "*Comme les fleurs!* Like the flowers! The same colors!"

"*Oui*, thank you," I say and she hands me the bag and I hold it against myself. All mine and lying in my arms, a little piece of France.

"What a beautiful day," I say out loud on the way home with my flowers and my clutch of licorice fennel in my basket. I am already imagining cutting out an orange silk dress with velvet sleeves and a red velvet panel down the front. It will fit me. And it will have the biggest silk sash around the dropped waist. It will be a glorious version of that doll dress. And when I pass the kiosk with the poster of Windel leaning over his piano, I just look away.

Chapter 15

In the hallway outside our double doors, I hear voices, chatter, laughter, singing. I step into the apartment and call out, "Mom?"

First thing I see is Logan slouching on the loveseat in the salon. Just over his head in another tapestry stands Louis the Sixteenth, Dad's favorite French king, probably because he was chubby like Dad.

Ava sweeps around and flops down next to Logan. My younger-sister heart drops a few notches.

I stand in front of them, reminding myself of one of Snow White's seven dwarves, Bashful.

"Hey, Petunia Beanly! Pretty girl," Logan says.

"You look bedraggled," says Ava. "What's in the bag?"

"Oh, nothing, Ava," I say.

"Hey, that's some jacket," says Logan. "I've never seen one like that before."

"I made it myself," I say sort of quietly, still standing in front of the two of them. I look down at the rug. "I make all my clothes and their patterns. But Mom doesn't really think they are practical."

"They are pretty funny, aren't they?" Ava says, laughing. "And she wears these things everywhere. I mean, silk blouses to soccer practice, to take out the garbage, to walk the dog."

"Are we talking about stuffed dogs, Ava?" I say.

"No, we aren't," says Ava, frowning at me.

"Oh, because if we are, I should tell you that Ava had to bring her stuffed dog with her on the plane. She fuzzes his ears when she's sad," I say with a big younger-sister smile on my face. Then I look down and keep my head that way.

"Really?" says Logan. "A stuffed dog? But that's so sweet. I like dogs too. Ava, what's his name?"

"Puppy," says Ava, biting her lip. "I know it's not a very original name but he just has this cute little lost look on his face and all I can think of is Puppy when I look at him. And Pet forgot to tell you she sucked her thumb until she was nine years old."

"Eight," I say, cringing.

"And Pet, Windel Watson is in Paris," says Ava with her twinkling eyes on me. "You know, the boy Pet stalked to the edge of the earth this spring. She stalked him so badly that he almost had to go into the witness protection program."

"Ava! I did not," I say and I feel a fiery sadness.

"You stalked Windel?" says Logan. "Really?"

"Um, well," I say.

"You know, my mom has a homemade CD of one of his songs. And she plays that thing all the time," says

Logan. He settles back with his arm almost around Ava. *Oh, don't put it around her. Don't!*

Logan has just gotten a haircut so he has a fresh-scrubbed, pink-eared little-boy look about him. I love the way all boys get that look after a haircut. Even my dad.

"Oh yeah," says Ava. "I remember the CD. It circulated around school for a while. Supposedly he wrote the song for Erin Barslow. Everybody liked Erin last year, even Jared Baker from my class."

"Erin Barslow?" I say, feeling breathless. "Um, Windel wrote her a song?"

"Logan, you didn't say anything about the dress *I'm* wearing. I sewed this myself too. My seams are perfect. I used a McCall pattern. Pet can't even use a bought pattern. She can't do it," says Ava.

"I could if I wanted, Ava," I say.

"I doubt that," she says. "And the insides of her dresses are a mess, with threads everywhere." Ava looks down at her own dress. It is black and sleeveless. She smooths the skirt. Then she sniffs and looks up.

"Ava, you know what? My mom helps out at the embassy every year when they do this fashion show. It's only for American students and it's kind of a big deal. Hard to get into but you should try out. My mom has a stack of applications at home. It's just for Americans. No, I mean it," says Logan.

"What about me?" I say.

"You're too young, Pet," says Ava. "That show is only for high school kids, right, Logan?"

"Yeah, probably," says Logan. "But not to worry. Hey, why don't you play some Scrabble with us? Though I have to warn you, there's nothing left but a bunch of O's."

"Oh," I say.

"Yeah, lots of those," says Logan and he gives me a smile, an ice cream smile with blue and yellow and green sprinkles all over the top.

I look at him and I feel kind of faint. Jean-Claude says the way to say "I fainted" in French translates as "I fell in the apples." I am definitely in the apples right now.

"Actually, we're pretty much done with Scrabble. And I was just reading Ava a little bit of this book, *Catcher in the Rye*," says Logan. "In French it's called *The Catcher of Hearts*."

"Funny," says Ava, looking down and whispering. "Because that's just what *you* are, Logan."

"I read that book twice," I say. "And Ava hasn't read it at all."

Suddenly Ava gets up and leans her head back and says, "Logan, look. I think my hair has grown since we've been here. It's below my waist. Can you believe it? Look. Logan, tell me. Look."

Mom is calling me so I take my flowers and I go into the kitchen thinking, *Why am I too young for the fashion show*? And, *Oh . . . Windel Watson wrote a song for Erin Barslow*.

I am just putting the orange and red tulips in a vase when Ava announces that she's walking Logan home and I shout out, "Hey, wait for me!" I run back into the salon. But Logan and Ava are already gone.

The Scrabble game didn't get put away. Then I see someone has arranged wooden letters on the table to form two words. It reads: "ERIN BARSLOW."

Chapter 16

For the last two nights, I sat on the balcony in the moonlight, stitching. On the table, there are two little sparkly candles that I lit. I worked and worked on the orange-and-maroon velvet dress. As it slowly emerged in my hands, I realized it looked so much like the doll dress. Of course, I was wishing I had a sewing machine. Ava found one for ten euros somewhere but I don't get to use it.

As I stitched I just kept thinking about Erin Barslow and how Windel wrote her that song. It figures.

This morning in my room I look at the orange-and-maroon velvet dress and I decide it's done. So I put the dress on. Then I open the armoire doors and look into the mirror at myself wearing it.

Suddenly I stand back. I have been so busy making the dress that I haven't even thought about *why* a doll dress might be hidden away for so many years. I mean the doll dress must be at least a hundred years old. Why would it *need* to be hidden?

When I finish a dress I usually like to wear it immediately, no matter what. An outfit can become "too dressy" very quickly if it sits in your closet too long, and once it becomes "too dressy," if you have my kind of life, it is a lost cause. So at least I would like to wear it downstairs to get the mail.

I open my door and stick my head out into our hall. I don't want Mom to see me. She will really hate this one. It's by far my weirdest dress yet. "Dad will like it," I say, nodding to myself because suddenly I am not sure if *I* like my new dress. A worried feeling pours over me.

It's very quiet this morning. Everyone is still asleep. I tiptoe into the dark hall, trying to imagine *why* someone would go to the trouble of locking away a little doll dress. Then I hear a noise. I freeze.

I back up slowly and I step right smack into Ava. She's standing there wearing her dog pajamas.

"Where are you going in *that*?" says Ava. "That is just plain weird."

"It is?" I say.

"Yes," says Ava. "Very."

"Ava," I say, standing up as tall as I can. "Maybe you don't know this, but style is risk taking. Style is wearing silk and velvet to a French 'fooootball' game . . . and not caring if everybody looks at you sideways." I return her flat stare.

Page forty-eight: In tight spaces, do the Little Sister Shuffle. This tends to confuse the older sibling.

So I start to do a little early morning dance right in front of Ava.

"What are you doing? Why don't you just give up?" says Ava. She folds her arms. There are dogs with red bows printed all over her flannel sleeves.

"This dress is my style, Ava. Maybe you don't understand, but style is walking through the Café Oui in a plaid silk dress with cowboy boots on and yes, a backpack and a baseball cap, while listening to Dad lecture about some dead French novelist. Style is standing by whatever you do and not backing down!" I say, still kind of doing the Little Sister Shuffle. Then, by mistake, I trip over the vacuum cleaner that somebody left in the hall. I fall on my face.

"What style!" says Ava, laughing.

When I get to my feet, I take a few twirls in the dress, even though I sort of feel like crying. But it doesn't spin away the hurt. I just feel dizzy on top of everything else. I look down at my dress. It used to seem so pretty to me.

I head for the mailboxes in the downstairs hall. The concierge has her door open. She spots me peering in our mailbox . . . "Oh, *non non non*, no letters," she calls from her couch in front of her TV. "*Le courrier n'est pas arrivé.* There is *une grève*, a strike. There will be no mail now."

Oh, maybe this is why I haven't heard from Ginger since we got here, why she didn't warn me about Windel's French tour occurring so quickly, leaving me gasping for air on the streets of Paris when I saw the poster.

The concierge comes out of her apartment. (Dad calls it her "lair.") She begins rearranging papers on the hall table. Then she looks up at me and stops still.

Her eyes freeze on me and her face is suddenly filled with terror. Then it changes to turmoil. "Where did you get this?" she whispers. "The dress? I can't believe it." Tears fill her eyes.

"I made it," I said. "I sewed it. I . . ." And then I feel terrible all over again. Maybe Ava is right, I should just give up. Why did I so foolishly get Jean-Claude to pick the lock on that drawer? Does the concierge know? Yes, I opened someone else's gift. But I mean, it was an *old* gift. Is there an unspoken expiration date on somebody else's present?

"Madame, I . . ."

"Non. Non," says the concierge. "It can't be. I am surely dreaming. It is not possible." And she goes into her apartment and closes her door. Since my family arrived in Paris, I have *never* seen her door shut.

Chapter 17

I stare at Madame's closed door. The maroon and orange tulips and the maroon-and-orange doll dress swirl around in my mind, as if floating in Ginger's crystal ball. *Maybe you should just give up.* "No!" I say out loud.

Suddenly I start knocking on the concierge's door. Quietly at first and then louder. I don't stop. Finally I hear the sound of a latch and the concierge pokes her head out. "Madame, um," I say. "Um . . ."

The concierge looks at my dress. She touches one of the velvet sleeves. She looks into my face.

"Please," I say. "I didn't mean to do anything wrong."

She looks at the velvet sash. She closes her eyes and when she opens them, a wash of sadness pours over her face. "Perhaps I am dreaming. Perhaps. *Oui. Peut-être.* Perhaps you are only a dream little girl. A mirage. But you come with me anyway," she says.

I follow Madame as she raps on Monsieur Le Bon Bon's door. Then she turns the handle and goes in with her nose leading the way.

Monsieur Le Bon Bon's apartment is dark except in the kitchen, where Albert perches in his cage set before a bright window.

The concierge goes straight for the bedroom. Monsieur Le Bon Bon is lying in his bed. She throws open his curtains. "*Bon courage*, Le Bon Bon!" She says. "Have courage!"

Monsieur stares at the ceiling. "I have brought the little girl from the Barbour apartment. *Voilà!* Look!"

"*Bonjour!*" I say. Monsieur Le Bon Bon continues to study the ceiling.

"You see, he won't get out of bed. It's because he lost his love. This woman has chosen a man who sells hams," says the concierge, pulling the white sheet up to Monsieur Le Bon Bon's chin and then tucking and smoothing it around him.

"Le Bon Bon understands English," she goes on, "but he doesn't admit it! You tell him, Petunia. Tell him there are other women in the sea."

"You mean other fish in the sea," I say.

"Yes, there are other fish in the sea," says Madame. "There are lots of fish everywhere. Lots of fish who would marry a nice monsieur. Isn't that so, Petunia?"

"Yes," I say. "Um, sort of."

"Come," she says, patting the foot of Monsieur Le Bon Bon. "Albert is hungry. You must get out of bed!"

For some reason Monsieur Le Bon Bon's foot poking up under the white sheet makes me feel sad. The concierge keeps patting his foot. "This little girl knows something about *ma grand-mère*. My *petite* grandmother. You know? This one has seen something, I think. Look at what she is wearing!" Suddenly Madame puts her head in her hands and begins crying.

"Oh, I didn't mean any harm," I say again. "Please! I am so sorry."

Suddenly Monsieur Le Bon Bon sits up in bed as if Madame's tears have brought him back to life. "She wants to know," says Monsieur Le Bon Bon in a very thick accent. "She wants to know about the dress. You make that? Tell her. Tell her!"

Chapter 18

The concierge goes to the windows in Monsieur Le Bon Bon's bedroom and she pushes them open and out. The courtyard is beyond and the sun is speckling the floor. And shadows from the green plane trees startle and stutter across the cobblestones. The doves are cooing above the window ledge and the nightingale is singing its string of notes at the top of the trees. I still haven't seen the nightingale. I only hear it. Madame brings Albert and his cage to the bedroom. Then she sits in a shaft of sunlight near the open French windows.

"The dress you have made reminds me of something," she says. "You understand?" Then she closes her eyes and adds in a soft, hesitating way. "He wants me to tell you the story of my grandmother."

"Oh yes," I say. "Please."

"First you will get out of bed, Le Bon Bon? They will not hold your job forever," she says. "It's a good job. You must go back."

"Peut-être," he says with his head tucked down into the sheets. "Perhaps."

"Ah, first he must have a glass of water. Can you get it for him?" she says.

I go and get a glass of water for Monsieur Le Bon Bon. Then I sit down and wait. Finally the concierge sighs and begins, "You see, my grandmother's name was Delphine Rouette. The name Delphine is linked to the delphinium flower. It's a flower name like Petunia. And she was always little, like you too. *Elle était toute petite! Toute petite!* Like you. She never grew very tall."

Monsieur Le Bon Bon looks sadly at me and shakes his head. Then he sits up against his pillow and nods along as the concierge speaks, as if he knows already what she will be saying. She opens the cage and holds out her fingers and Albert grabs one and sits up high on it. As she strokes his green and orange and purple feathers, she says, "My grandmother, when she was twelve years old, worked with her mother at home, the way children did in those days. Children often had to string beads or sew buttons on cards or stitch together strips of straw for hats. They were paid a small amount for each piece completed. Today all children go to school. But back then, no, many worked instead. I do not think our Jean-Claude could have managed that. Do you, Le Bon Bon?"

Monsieur Le Bon Bon puffs out his cheeks, blows air through his teeth, and says, "*Mais non! Pas du tout!* No!"

"You see, my little grandmother had a great talent. Even though she was only twelve years old, she was a magnificent seamstress." The concierge whispers when she says this. "Perhaps a little bit like you. Her mother was a great couturier. What is a couturier, you are thinking? I will tell you. It is a grand seamstress and dressmaker. But they did not design and sew clothes for people to wear. No, no, no, *les robes étaient toutes petites*! So little! They made *doll* dresses. They worked for Madame Ernestine Jumeau and the Jumeau doll company in Paris. This was the most famous French company of all. Here in Paris were the workshops and stores that sold the dresses and the beautiful dolls. This was my little Delphine Rouette in the 1890s, my small grandmother."

Monsieur Le Bon Bon has a little tear on his cheek and he tilts his head to the side as the concierge speaks.

"Delphine had been allowed to sew only the underclothes for the dolls, the slips and the bloomers. The children who worked for the factory were not allowed to sew the fancy dresses. Every week Delphine and her mama would visit Madame Jumeau at the workshop to show her the new dresses the mother had made and all the slips and bloomers that Delphine had sewn. Madame Jumeau would either approve of them and place orders for more or she would reject them. It was always up to Madame Jumeau.

"Although most beloved of all companies, the Jumeau doll company had a problem. Because they were so admired, because they were the best doll company in France and in all the world, other companies were jealous. German doll companies wanted to outdo the Jumeau dolls. They wanted to destroy the company. They wanted to copy the exquisite dresses and sell them at much cheaper prices. And so they installed a spy in the workshops of Madame Ernestine Jumeau.

"Around this time there was a big World's Fair coming up. It was to be in Chicago in the United States. The Jumeau doll company would be featured in the new women's pavilion. They would have an enormous glass vitrine, a huge display case in the center of the building. The company was in great excitement and great activity. You see, it was very important. All the seamstresses and couturiers in Paris who worked for Madame Jumeau wanted to create a dress that would be accepted by Madame Jumeau and sent to this big fair. Such excitement! Such anticipation, you cannot imagine.

"Madame Jumeau and her team of seamstresses planned the special outfits for all the dolls. But what about the spy? No one knew who it was. How could they keep the spy from seeing the new dresses?

"One afternoon when Delphine went with her mama to the workshops of Ernestine Jumeau, Madame Jumeau took them aside. She whispered to Delphine's mama, 'As you plan a new dress for the big World's Fair coming up, *don't bring it here*. I do not know who the spy is. She could be anyone among us.'

"The spy was probably a woman because only women and girls worked for the Jumeau company, with a few exceptions. 'Please,' Madame Jumeau whispered, 'bring the dresses wrapped in tissue to the Luxembourg Gardens.'

She pressed a tiny key in my great-grandmother's hand. 'There is a little hidden box inside the marble pedestal behind the statue of the cupid standing over the pond. You know the pond tucked among the roses. Unlock the little box and set the dresses within. Lock it back up and I will come and pick them up after dark.'

"Ernestine Jumeau looked around her workshop at all the faces of the women and girls who worked for her. Some were in shadows and some in sunlight. Some were dressing dolls in lace costumes. Some were preparing them to go into their boxes and others were sewing last-minute buttons on dresses. Some were carrying bolts of printed silk ordered from Lyon. Others unrolled crisp checked cotton onto the worktables.

"Madame Jumeau sighed and put her arm around my great-grandmother and her daughter Delphine. 'I know I can trust you two. I will keep all the doll dresses that will be considered for the fair. I will pick the best for the show. But I do not want the spy to see any of these dresses. These will remain a secret. And I will make my selection in private.'

"Delphine and my great-grandmother left the workshops of the Jumeau doll company. They walked home wondering and worrying. Who could the spy be?"

Now the concierge looks at me. Her eyes fade from lavender to a blue gray behind her almost tears. And her curly, henna-colored hair seems softened by the story and the filtered light in the bedroom. She looks at me for a long time and then she puts her face in her hands again. "The dress you are wearing. It reminds me. It reminds me. It is so like something."

"Oh, I am very sorry," I say. "I didn't realize. I . . . I wouldn't have . . . But who was the spy?"

"Ah yes, the spy," says the concierge. And more sadness and clouds fill her eyes. She pulls a lacy handkerchief from her pocket. "Call me Collette, *ma chérie*. Since I see you wearing that dress, it feels as if you have come here as if sent by my grandmother herself. Tell me how you came to sew it." She takes my hand and squeezes it tightly.

I pull back a little, feeling torn. Should I mention the present I so thoughtlessly opened? Will the concierge be angry with me for breaking a lock and then opening a gift that was not mine? And did we not swear to secrecy, Jean-Claude and I?

Just then Dad is calling me. I hear his hurry-up voice echoing in the hall. "All set! Petunia, we're ready to go out!" I look at the concierge whose name is Collette and I feel a terrible urge to tell her about the doll dress. But there is too much to explain and not enough time. I take a few steps backward and say, "Um, my family is going somewhere. I'll come back later. Okay? Bye! *Merci!*" And I wave to Monsieur Le Bon Bon and to Collette.

I rush to the door but I turn around and look back just before I leave. Collette is now sitting with Monsieur Le Bon Bon on the edge of his bed. Le Bon Bon is opening his mouth like a baby bird and Collette is putting drops of vitamins on his tongue with a small medicine dropper.

Chapter 19

I find Mom and Ava sitting on the staircase. Ava has stubbed her toe and Mom is leaning over her.

"Oh, Mom. I'm just going to change my dress, okay? Don't worry. I won't wear this outside," I say, scooting by them.

Dad shakes his head at me in wonder. "Pet," he says, "another dress! Wow! Just look at that!" My dad kind of follows me partway upstairs. Everything amazes my dad.

"Dad, you were going to run down and buy me a Band-Aid, remember?" says Ava, looking up at Dad with those green pond eyes, full of pain.

"Oh, sure, sweetheart, Pumpkin. I was just . . . I'll go right now," says Dad, bumbling forward.

I hurry up to our floor. I rush into our apartment and change into jeans, because that's what Mom wants.

Then, checking that I am truly alone, I creep quietly into Ava's room. This is a tactic I am used to taking. I mean, if I didn't do this, I would have *no idea* what Ava is up to. That could be dangerous. I cut past Ava's perfectly made bed. I mean, you could bounce a euro on that thing it's tucked so tightly. I slide toward her dresser, the natural landing place for papers. And *there* it is, the announcement of the fashion show and the rules and all that. The fashion show is called “Sew, You’re in Paris!” I knew it! Ava got this when she walked Logan home that afternoon.

I look at the guidelines quickly. Hmmm. And I don’t see anything about age mentioned. Hmmm. You just have to be an American student. I slip the paper in my jeans pocket.

This is an ordinary day in a younger-sister’s life. This is common practice. This is nothing more than typical survival tactics of a second born.

Chapter 20

As we troop down the rue Michel-Ange, Mom and Ava with arms locked together, me and Dad bumbling behind, Dad announces that we are going to the Luxembourg Gardens. It's true he has been talking about this for days. Still when he says those words *Luxembourg Gardens*, I feel almost like laughing or hiccupping. As soon as you take note of something, it begins popping up everywhere. Like the time Ginger announced she was sleepy when her mom was driving me home. And just about a minute later we passed a turnoff and a signpost that said "Sleepy Road." Everybody in the van laughed, especially Ginger's mom, who chalks up stuff like that to *the beautiful spook of everything.* "We're all connected," she always says to Ginger. "And we're not supposed to know it. But sometimes there's a little hole or rip in the cloth of life and we see by mistake. I am reading palms later today, Pet. Interested? I can do you a freebie."

The Luxembourg Gardens are a deep emerald green, a waxy dark green. And as we walk through the gate, I say, "Dad, I don't want to go in the Luxembourg Palace. I just want to sit on this bench until you guys get back. Okay?"

Dad hesitates but my mom and Ava pull him forward. Soon he's chugging along, the cheese in between two slices of bread. I wave to them. When they go around some clipped bushes, I take off. I have to find a copy shop. Now!

I hurry, passing a mossy pool in the garden where a marble cupid stands watching over its murkiness. This must be the very pool Delphine Rouette and her mama moved toward carrying a small parcel of doll dresses wrapped in tissue.

In my mind, I see them in their long skirts tripping past me, looking behind themselves in a nervous way, being cautious about the spy who might be following them. Then they go over to the cupid and kneel behind him to find the hidden box.

Suddenly I too work my way through the tangle of rosebushes and damp white blossoms. I get up close to the cupid, who stands luminous and shining among the leaves. Why was the little dress hidden in the drawer all those years? And what is it that makes the concierge cry? The cupid, softened by rain and wind, stands above me. His face seems to know everything. But since he is made of stone, his mouth is frozen in time and he cannot tell me.

Chapter 21

Now I hurry out through the park gates and along the boulevard. I have no idea where I might find a copy shop. Whizzing and oblivious French cars rush past me. Then along a construction wall I see another one of the Windel Watson posters. My heart sinks again. How much farther can it drop? Does Erin Barslow play the piano too? Is she in town as well?

I am standing here with the Parisian wind, warm and swaying around me, the leaves speaking an unknown language, clicking together, whispering. Suddenly I see Madame la concierge walking down the street toward me. She seems to be part of the wind, her shopping bags billowing.

"Madame!" I call out.

"But here you are!" she says, sailing toward me.

"You too," I say. "And so far from our building."

"Oh, you know, I walk," says the concierge, looking down. "And I had some things to do nearby."

"Gee, I was hoping there was a copy shop around here," I say, the application in my hand fluttering in the wind. "I have something I need to copy."

"Yes, I see that. What are you applying for?" she says.

"Oh, um, a fashion show," I say.

"Ah," says the concierge.

"I mean, it's a secret. I mean, Mom and Ava . . . But Logan said . . . I am not sure . . . so I am nervous, but . . ."

"Oh?" says Collette. "You know, there's a little store with a copy machine up on the corner two blocks down that way. I just walked by there."

"Oh my gosh. Thank you!" I say.

"*Mais bien sûr!* After all, my grandmother sent you, did she not?" says the concierge, smiling at me.

"No, I don't think so," I say, laughing a little.

But I feel a light twitch of wonder as the concierge walks away. She waves. I wave. Her shopping bags full of wind blow forward with her light coat flapping. So too, small green flower petals from the trees above lift and wash across the sidewalk. *The falling glitter of coincidence.*

Chapter 22

It's my job today to gather up all the dishes around the Barbours' apartment. So I venture into Dad's office. It is kind of a mess. He has about five cups of coffee sitting on his desk. I put the cups on a tray and set the tray by the door. I am just about to pick up some newspapers from the floor when I happen to look up at a framed drawing on Dad's wall. I take a deep breath and look again.

What? It's a pastel drawing of the Eiffel Tower in red. Red! Just like *my* drawing. "When the Eiffel Tower was first built, it was red," the lady at the bakery told me. "This is something you Americans in the States don't know."

I look at the drawing again. My heart tips over, crashes, tumbles. A tower of blocks smashing to the floor. The framed drawing is signed *Ava Beanly*.

"Mom!" I shout out and I go rushing through the apartment from room to room. "Mom!"

Mom is sitting at a small table on the shady balcony off the kitchen. She has some postcards she's written to friends at home scattered before her on the table. One of them says in her curly handwriting, *Feeling a little lost these days*.

Mom is looking down into the courtyard below. From here the plane trees seem to form a thick canopy of green, blocking the view. Maybe Collette is sitting down there with Albert the parrot. I wish I could see them.

"Mom!" I pull on her sleeve. "Mom, Ava copied my Eiffel Tower drawing. She saw it in my room. She copied it!"

"Oh, Pet, you are the living limit! Angus really likes Ava's drawing. She framed it for him, for goodness' sake. Please don't spoil that," says Mom.

"Mom!" I say. "But . . ."

"Pet!" says Mom. "Angus hung it up right near his desk! Ava was just so proud of that. And I was proud *for* her."

"Oh," I say, backing up. I pause for a moment in the doorway. I look at my mom. She seems so far away with her head turned and all her postcards spread out before her.

Chapter 23

This afternoon Monsieur Le Bon Bon has gotten out of bed and is taking Jean-Claude home on his bicycle. Jean-Claude rides on the handlebars, waving at me as I stand on the front balcony. "I am going home now but don't forget to visit Albert while I am gone," he calls. "He is my great love, next to you. Maybe I even love Albert more." Jean-Claude throws me kisses from the rickety handlebars.

"Hold on to the bicycle, Jean-Claude," I call back.

"Do we still have our little secret together? Something only you and I share?" he shouts.

"Shhh, Jean-Claude," I yell back. "No we don't, okay? Bye." The bicycle wobbles off down the street. Monsieur Le Bon Bon keeps smiling and not looking straight ahead, and a tiny three-wheeled truck screeches around them. I stand here worrying as they disappear.

The balcony smells of Ava's suntan lotion. Ava's towel is draped over a chair and her magazines are splashed around. It feels like Ava's balcony. I have a sinking suspicion the whole world belongs to Ava too and perhaps there is no room for me *anywhere*. I will *not* cry.

Logan stopped by to pick up Ava a while ago. He told me he was taking Ava to visit a tiny old sweet shop where some say Marie Antoinette used to order little pastel bonbons over two hundred years ago. Then Ava showed Logan the framed Eiffel Tower drawing that she did. I just stood there in the hall near the landline phone and didn't say anything.

But that pressing feeling is bothering me. And I guess I have a case of the Beanly blues. At least I can go to visit Collette. I'll probably show her the doll dress I found. I do not know what she will say or do about the whole thing so I am nervous.

I go to my armoire and pick up the little dress. The velvet is so soft, the silk so delicate. Every tiny stitch seems to be a part of a story, the story the little dress must tell me. I wrap it up and tuck it into my backpack.

As I look around my room, I have a feeling someone has been in here. It just feels like things are moved around a little bit. For instance, the scissors are lying in a different way on my table. Oh but maybe I just forgot how I left them. I feel unsure here in Paris of everything. I don't understand anything; even my room baffles me.

I shake off the chill that flutters up my back. Then I am off down the hall and out the double doors past Dad, who is vacuuming the rug in the outer hall. Dad loves to vacuum. Nothing makes him happier than plugging in that noisy machine and sucking around corners and under chairs with it. Mom loves to direct him. "Angus, over there! You missed that part of the rug!"

When I get down to the foyer I hear another distinct sound coming from Collette's apartment. It reminds me of a train chugging along a steep track. I lean through her open door. "Madame!" I call out. And then I add with a meeker voice, "I mean, Collette! *Vous êtes là?*" I attempt to say in French "Are you there?" I mean, oops, I probably got that wrong.

But then I hear, *"Oui! Ici, ma chérie, viens ici."*

Collette is calling me. I follow the noise of the train, the hum, the roar, and I realize as I get closer, it is the sound of a sewing machine humming along.

I wind my way through the clutter, following the sound until I get to a room that opens onto the courtyard. Collette is sitting at a sewing machine. She nods at me.

"*Bonjour!* Yes, I am sewing. You have inspired me. I haven't sewn in a long time. I am making a, how do you say, shirt and *une cravate*, a necktie for Le Bon Bon. He won't find a woman to love him dressed in his worn-out suit. It has holes at the elbows. No woman likes to see elbows like that. I told him. But you know what? He refuses! He refuses to go to a boutique to buy a new one. He is too shy. So I will sew him a shirt and necktie *en soie*! In silk. Can a woman resist a shy man in a silk shirt? No. No. Never!"

"I love to sew," I say, "but everything I do is weird and nobody likes my dresses. Not even me, I guess. But I found the copy shop. Thanks for that."

"*Mais oui!*" says the concierge, looking at me carefully. "Have you ever heard of Coco Chanel? She was a little bit different too. Her clothing designs ended up changing women's fashion forever. Do you think it is good to create things that look like everybody else's?"

"Um, I don't know," I say.

She pats the seat of the chair beside her and I sit down. "Did you know that Le Bon Bon can dance the swing?" she says. "Oh yes! But he won't go to the Hôtel Magique, where they have music for dancing. Too shy! I will have to go along and, you know, I am seventy-nine years old. Not a baby kitten! But I know the *patron*. He will help Le Bon Bon."

"The Hôtel Magique?" I say.

"Yes, where people dance!" says Collette, pushing her foot down on the treadle. The machine begins to roar along. The silky shirt collects the light as it lies on the table.

"This is an old machine. You know, of course, *to whom* it once belonged?" she says. "Ah, I worked very hard to understand your *whoms* and your *whos* when I studied your English! It is the most confusing language of all. It makes no sense."

"Did this sewing machine once belong to Delphine and her mama?" I say.

"*Oui.* Yes," says Collette. "Isn't it beautiful with all these gold and red flowers painted all over it?" Then she pauses and puts her face in her hand and sighs. "*Oh mon*

Dieu! *Oh mon Dieu*! Sometimes I cannot bear to think. Sometimes I cannot bear to remember."

"Oh, Collette, was it the spy? Did something happen because of the spy?" I say.

"Oh, there are things I have told no one. Even though it is worse to not talk about things, you know that, Petunia? Things can grow bigger in the dark, I mean if you don't bring them out, like clothes on the line. They must see the sun."

"I know," I say, thinking about Ava and all the things we never talk about, like her biological dad. *"You-know-who hurt me so much when he left me,"* Mom often says to Ava. *"So, let's just forget him, shall we?"* Ava always nods her head in agreement, staying loyal to Mom.

"You see, Petunia, when I saw you in that dress, I knew! I knew you had come to me. You had come to me for a reason. When I saw you in orange silk and maroon velvet I must confess I nearly died."

"You hated it," I say. "Like Mom and Ava."

"I did not hate it at all, *ma chérie. Pas du tout!!!* It's just that it reminded me of . . ." says Collette. "Oh, never mind, child. Never mind. *Bon courage!* Have courage, as we say here. I would like to offer you the use of my sewing machine. I can show you how to use the treadle. You push up and down with your feet. No electricity is needed."

"Oh, Madame!" I say.

"Collette!" she says.

"Oh, Collette! *Merci! Merci!*" I say, jumping up and down.

"Sit!" She pats my chair. She pours me a glass of water. "Drink!" she says. She pauses. She looks down and then she begins.

"You know, long ago the preparations for the important World's Fair in Chicago were very elaborate. All the couturiers in Paris who worked for the Jumeau doll company were designing and planning the most fabulous doll dresses, hoping their dress would be chosen. Of course Ernestine Jumeau herself was constantly working on the costumes for the dolls. Delphine's mama too planned a magnificent dress and she had begun to cut out the pieces of satin on the worktable at home. All the while, Delphine sewed buttons on the slips and bloomers.

"But every time her mama went out to the pâtisserie to buy a *tarte aux pommes* for their little breakfast, Delphine would set out her fabrics and the pattern she had made while no one was watching. She would remove the size eight Jumeau doll from the cabinet loaned to her mama for sizing dresses. She would try a sleeve or part of the blouse on the doll, to test the size. She worked with tiny stitches in secret because her *maman*, of course, would not allow her to break the rules at the Jumeau doll company."

"Children were not allowed to sew the fancy dresses?" I say.

"*Oui*, that is correct," says Collette. "*Oui. Oui. Oui.* And so Delphine worked on that little dress when no one was at home. In secret. She used both hand stitching and, in some parts, the sewing machine.

"But she was indeed a child. And children must play from time to time. On Sundays in the hot summer Delphine would go to swim in the Seine river. Like any child, like you, *ma petite.* There she often saw her dear stepsister, Sylvie. Delphine was very close to Sylvie. After all, they had grown up together. Delphine did not see her much now that her *maman* had separated from Sylvie's papa. Sylvie and her papa lived on the other side of Paris. But Delphine and her sister were able to swim together on Sundays. And even though they were both twelve years old, they always brought their little rag dolls with them.

"Today no one is allowed to swim in the Seine but back then they used to have sand for a beach and families would come to picnic and swim right there in the river. Look. I have a photograph here of Delphine and her dear sister wearing wool bathing suits, swimming in the Seine. To me, these bathing suits look like wool dresses! But it was a different time, was it not? This was the style."

Collette hands me the photograph, pointing out the rag doll in each of the girls' arms, and I look at the river behind them as she talks.

"Most of the time Delphine did not see her dear sister and she missed her. They mailed each other letters and waved to each other when they passed in halls at the Jumeau company. They were working children, you see.

"Sunday was the only day for play, the only day that Delphine did not work secretly on her doll dress. Every other day, every chance she got, she opened up her sewing basket and began to stitch and hem the tiny dress.

"When the little doll dress was nearly finished, Delphine looked at it and realized that it was very, *very* beautiful. She knew it was probably the most beautiful doll dress anyone had made in Paris that season."

"Do you know what color the dress was?" I ask.

Collette looks over at me. Her eyes have turned a distant bluish violet, like the perfume fields of Provence I have seen in a picture on her wall, dusky and far reaching under the French sunlight. "Yes, I know the colors," she says. "Yes, the little dress was made of orange silk and dark red velvet with the tiniest stitches made by a young girl's tiny hands."

"Did it look like this?" I say. I reach into my backpack and pull out the tissue and I set the little dress before her.

"*Oh mon Dieu! Mon Dieu!*" Collette cries out. "My grandmother made it! I haven't seen this dress since I was ten years old!" And she takes the dress in her hands and begins to cry. "I knew it. I knew it! My grandmother sent you. You have brought back the precious little dress, the dress that started everything. This dress too changed the course of my life," Collette says and then she cries quietly. I reach out and touch her arm.

Finally she is still. She dries her eyes. She sits up straight. "It is just exactly as I remember it," she says, putting the doll dress on the table. "I need to be alone now, *ma chérie. Oui.* I must. Leave this dress here. I will loan you another doll dress from the workshops of Ernestine Jumeau. I do not know who made this dress." Collette opens a cupboard and hands me another little doll dress. "This one is made of pink striped cotton with red trim and two pockets in the front and a sash across the waist. It's another little doll dress under the label of Jumeau. Perhaps it will inspire you to sew another dress for yourself. Here, take it and then, *oui*, I must be alone. Alone."

Chapter 24

When I leave Collette's apartment she asks me to shut her door tightly and I do. And then I go out of the building to the front steps. I sit on the top one, thinking about Delphine's little doll dress, letting the sun warm me. There is an archway there before our building, and climbing over the arch is a lanky, thick wisteria vine, which has just bloomed. Pale purple flowers hang as if heavy with sleep and dreams and too much sun. Birds flutter in and out among its branches and leaves.

Suddenly, just under the wisteria, I see Logan. His face is in leafy shadows. I startle and call out to him, but he turns and walks quickly away as if he doesn't hear me. As if he is caught up in something else, something far away. I go out onto the sidewalk and watch him almost sprinting like a running shadow down the street. As soon as he gets to the corner, he disappears. He didn't recognize me. It was as if he didn't know me at all. "Logan?" I call out along the street. Nothing answers but the wind.

I go back into the darkness of the hallway. The tiles on the floor are chilly and I think about how old they must be. I wonder if Delphine Rouette and her sister, Sylvie, walked on these very tiles.

I stop by the table to pick up *Le Monde* newspaper, which gets delivered for the Barbour apartment every day. Dad loves *Le Monde* and reads it in the evening, leaving Mom to sit near him and ask, "Anything about home in there? Just anything at all about America?"

I pick up the newspaper and tuck it under my arm along with the doll dress Collette loaned me. Then I see something. Something. There it is. Crisp and bright and white. An envelope. A letter addressed to Ava. *Ginger leans forward in my mind. Her blond curls fall over the blue crystal ball before her. The envelope lies in its murkiness. Clouds form around it. Ginger waves her hands. No, she says. No!*

I look again at the envelope on the table. Its brightness shines like a terrible beacon right through me. It slices like a laser beam. It is hand lettered. Hand delivered. *To Ava Beanly.* It's a letter from Logan. He brought it here and then slipped away through the wisteria. Michael the angel lifting over Paris, vanishing at the end of the rue Michel-Ange.

I grab the letter. I grab it, knowing it is wrong. Ava is sleeping unaware upstairs, lost in a golden older-sister nap, sure that all is well in her kingdom. I put the letter in my backpack. And I ride the elevator up to our apartment because my heart feels so heavy I could never pull it up all those stairs.

Chapter 25

I go immediately into the *salle de bain*, the yellow room with the long, deep bathtub in it. I turn on the hot water. It steams and sneezes and snuffles, as if to say, *"Mais pourquoi vous me dérangez maintenant?"* Why are you bothering me now? It snorts and complains and then it begins to putter along cheerfully, like everything in Paris.

Finally steam starts to rise from the tub and I hold Logan's envelope over it, loosening the glue carefully. *Ginger, please tell my planets I am sorry. Tell them to forgive me! Please ask the stars in the sky, the ones that are in alignment with me, please ask them to be gentle, to shine kindly on me with forgiveness.* It is not easy to be a younger sister, to be partially unwanted when you arrive by the other small person in your world. It is not easy to feel your very existence crowds this other older child. Forgive my heart line and my head line. Forgive the moons of Saturn in my fourth house. Forgive whatever galaxies have spun into my arc of despair. But I *have* to know. I have to see what Logan has written to my older sister.

Dear Ava,

I haven't slept for a few days. I can't stop thinking about you. If this comes as a total shock just throw this letter away and forget about it. But maybe you feel something too????? I really need to know. I'll stay away until I hear from you.

Logan

Oh no. No. No. No. This can't be. I can't let this happen. Ava doesn't deserve Logan. She has been so awful to me. What about my ruined blue silk dress? What about my Eiffel Tower drawing?

And then an idea suddenly pinches me on the elbow. It crosses my mind that I might write a letter back, pretending to be Ava. After all, she has been so mean! It's only fair! And I can copy Ava's handwriting. Younger sisters often can do that sort of thing. I have written *Ava Beanly* hundreds of times in my notebooks, practicing for just such an occasion. And wanting my handwriting to be perfect and even like Ava's, instead of messy and all over the place, like mine.

Dear Logan,

Actually no, I have NO feelings for you at all. I am beautiful but vacant. I don't even appreciate my wonderful sister, Pet.

Yours cordially,

Ava Beanly

Oh, but I can't even believe an idea like that crossed my mind! I could never send a letter like that to Logan.

I am not to blame for these thoughts! Originally it didn't come naturally to me, any of this. Younger sisters arrive in the world loving all things, admiring our older sisters. Younger sisters come into the world willing to share and be dazzled and charmed by our older sisters' constant abilities! They can walk and talk while we cannot, which is very impressive. We lie there in our cage-like cribs unable to speak or walk and then after struggling for months, we figure out how to drag ourselves across the floor, while our older sisters dance on their toes around us.

Soon we begin to discover that they seem already to have nailed down the parents as theirs, like the furniture in the house, most of the toys, and much of the clothing (the things we wear are hand-me-downs originally given to *them* from dear friends of *theirs*). Everything belongs to them. And they walk around claiming and keeping track of their possessions. We arrive on the scene as uninvited guests who are allowed to merely *borrow* the parents and darling toys!

I look down at Logan's letter. I did not choose such underhanded tactics. They chose me out of necessity and survival!

I take the letter upstairs and I put it in a drawer in my room under a pile of silk scraps and I shut the drawer tightly. Now that letter from Logan will never see the light of day again.

I sit alone with my huge dark armoire, a kind of shadowy friend, my only friend in Paris. In the cracks inside I often find pieces of ribbon and snippets of lace, old leftovers from past dazzling lives of romance and love. Something I must accept will never be mine.

And then, being upset, I get out my sewing basket, my threads and needles and scissors and the little Jumeau dress Collette loaned me. I begin making sketches in my notebook, ideas for a dress, a taffeta dress so beautiful you could lose every care in the world while sewing it.

Chapter 26

Page fifty-eight: Younger sisters tend to make many more mistakes than the older sisters when it comes to love. This is simply due to a condition called Second-Born Doormat Syndrome, and to determine whether or not you have this, check to see if you have been stepped on lately.

Yes, after Valentine's Day and what happened, Ginger was getting worried. She offered to help me find Windel's lost coat. She texted everybody she knew: *A stray overcoat was sent home by mistake from Armand Kent Elementary please check closets.* And it was Ginger who finally located the thing. David Franklin's father had taken it home by mistake that night, even though David never wears anything but down parkas. We decided Mr. Franklin must be secretly from Planet X. And Ginger was kind enough to go and pick up the coat from the Franklins.

But then she got it in her head that I should return it directly to Windel.

"Me? Directly?" I said, cringing.

She suggested I put on Windel's big baggy overcoat and go to his house. She wanted me to ring the bell and stand there on the porch smiling and waving my big tweedy grandpa arms.

"No way, Ginger," I said.

I knew I couldn't handle such a bold and risky move. I just didn't have that kind of self-confidence. That is a firstborn, older-sister kind of maneuver, outside the realm of a younger-sister's capabilities. I plan to go into detail about that when I write the book *How to Be a Younger Sister.*

"Look," Ginger said. "You lost the coat. You gotta return it. Why not do it in a cute way?"

"Cute?" I said.

"Cute," she said. And so finally, after much balking, I agreed. I put on Windel's big woolen coat over several sweaters and two pairs of jeans so I would have something to keep me warm on the way home and I walked to his house. I stood there trembling on the porch and rang the bell. Ginger had said, "Be sure to smile and say 'Surprise!' when he opens the door."

Unfortunately, unlike Ava, neighborhood dogs have never liked me. As soon as I rang the bell, one of them came roaring and barking around the corner. It rushed at me with big teeth and wild ears flapping. And yes, I screamed. I dashed and jumped and sprinted. But I also tried to shout "Surprise!" as I scrambled and bolted down the steps. Sadly when Windel opened the door all he saw was this weird girl wearing his lost overcoat running off down the street. I mean, how much more could Windel endure? And I wouldn't blame him!

But on the positive side, Windel did finally get his coat back. Ginger mailed it to him with a note in the pocket that simply said *Sorry.*

Chapter 27

Logan's letter practically burns a hole in my head now. I keep sketching and sketching ideas for my new dress. And then I go out for a walk and circle the neighborhood streets. It is an Auteuil Market day and I buy a piece of striped silk. It is a tiny blue stripe, not pink like the little dress Collette loaned me.

Back in the building, I find Collette's door is still closed. And I stand for a minute leaning against it, as if putting my head on her shoulder.

When I get back to my room, I am sure someone has been in here again. I had tried to memorize the way I left the fabrics, the papers, even my scissors. Everything has been moved slightly. Was it the wind? I close the window. Then I start pinning the new silk onto the pattern I drew and I begin to cut the dress out.

I work all day on the dress until the Paris sky darkens and the lights of the city come on. The Eiffel Tower glows against the skyline. The young woman living across the street and opposite me becomes once again visible in her lit-up apartment. Perhaps she is just out of university and living alone for the first time. She has a large birdcage behind her full of small white birds. Finches maybe. I have never seen her in real life on the street below in the daytime. And yet there she is as soon as darkness falls.

Tonight as I work, the letter from Logan to Ava simmers in me like a pot of sorrowful soup. It bubbles and burns. Wretched Ava! No boy has ever returned my love! Not once!

On the other hand there is a part of me that is excited for Ava. A real boy is in love with *her*! Not some passing flirtation in a flower shop but a real boy in love! Part of me wants to rush to Ava and give her the letter and jump up and down for joy and excitement for her. But the nighttime, darker, hurt, and angry part of me holds on. Let the soup boil. Let it burn.

Sew. Sew. If I must be so awful, so dreadful in my heart, then I will make something beautiful to counteract it. To make up for the darkness, I will make pure light! A floaty pale blue, striped taffeta dress with pockets and an attached sash.

Dad went to London this afternoon to study something at the British Museum. He took the Chunnel. Mom was freaked about him going under the ocean. But then Mom is freaked about a lot of things. She didn't want to be alone in Paris without Dad. She can't sleep tonight. She's been walking up and down the hall. And Ava comes out of her room at around ten and asks if Logan has called.

"No," I say, "the phone hasn't rung at all." And then yards of guilt drop over me, a loosened bolt of the darkest, blackest silk. The letter in my drawer burns and cries and pulls and twists and tugs in me. And I keep sewing.

At ten thirty the phone rings. Mom rushes toward it from her bedroom, flying past my room like an angel in white. She lifts the receiver. It's heavy and old-fashioned. "Hello? Yes." Long silence. "What?" Another stretch of silence. "You are calling too often." Pause. "I see." Then she covers the receiver with her hand and whispers, "Pet, go in your room and close the door. This doesn't concern you." More silence, another long pause. "Well, I don't know how she'll feel. I think it's rather late tonight. But I will talk to her. Pet, close your door. Go back into your room."

Whenever Dad's away the house always feels darker. The Louis the Sixteenth furniture looks narrow and unkind and uncomfortable. The sky is a dark, foreign purple. The night closes in around us, turning everything into patterned moving shadows. The traffic hisses and water hisses through the pipes to someone else's sink in the apartment above us.

That was Ava's father calling again. The rain splashes and tears at the building. I saw Ava's birth certificate when we were applying for passports last year. One part she covered up with her hand but I saw it. Her last name wasn't Beanly. It said Ava Preston. Ava doesn't have Dad's last name. She has some other name. Is her biological father's name William Preston? The trees blow against the windows. The rain hits the glass and pours over it, blurring everything.

Mom hangs up the phone and calls Ava to the dining room. They shut the doors. I can hear muffled talking and then Ava crying. I can hear her call out, "But he's *not* my dad. Dad's my dad. I don't want to have ice cream crêpes with some stranger tomorrow or any other time. No!"

The wind rattles the shutters of the building. It's growing late. The girl across the street has covered up her birdcage and turned off her computer and she has disappeared into unseen hallways and unseen spaces, leaving a black vacant darkness in the room across from my window.

Chapter 28

Dad took the night train from London. He was all hyper and stealthy and snuck in at around seven this morning, while we were sleeping. Now he wants us all to have breakfast on the balcony. He has cooked scrambled eggs as a surprise. He walks around asking if there's a blue checked tablecloth in any of the drawers. "You know, like in the Bonnard painting?" he says.

"Honey, there isn't room for all of us out there," says Mom.

"Oh, come on! So we'll squeeze a little, Buddy. It's such a perfect Sunday morning for a French breakfast on the balcony!" Dad says, sort of barging in on the cobweb of gloom that settled over everything here while he was gone.

Last night was terrible, what with Ava's father calling and me trying to sleep with that letter floating around in my head. When I awoke in the middle of the night I saw that the girl across from my window was also awake and once again on her computer. She kept getting up and walking around in circles as if she too were in turmoil.

Dad is now carrying a tray to the balcony, the coffee in white bowls, a dish of eggs, a compote of jam. Next he produces a fresh baguette, pretends it is a baseball bat, holds it over his shoulder, and says, "Pitch it right in there, Pet!" And when no one laughs Dad looks suddenly awkward and shy.

Ava appears with a blanket wrapped around her shoulders. She looks like a butterfly going back into the cocoon stage. Since it is so sunny out, I have put on my big floppy green hat with the polka dots on the brim. "That's ridiculous," Ava says, looking at me. "It matches what?"

"Your blanket," I say and stare right back at her.

We all sit around the table with Mom squished against the wall. Bright red geraniums stretch from flower pots around us. The sun is shining, cheerful and perky and unaware, like Dad today. The bread is still warm. The sweet butter melts into it. The hot cocoa is creamy and light, Sunday church bells ring in the distance. Everything is welcome and warm, except for the motor scooters roaring along on the rue Michel-Ange and Ava's red swollen face and Logan's hidden letter.

Mom doesn't take her eyes off Ava. She even has her hand on Ava's arm and squeezes it a few times occasionally as if she's sending Ava a message in Morse code.

Ava, wrapped in her blanket, produces a stack of French patterns and puts them on the table. On the cover of each package is a chic teen modeling some short 1970s-looking dress.

"Honey, Ava is trying out for that fashion show at the embassy. Give her some kudos," says Mom.

"Kudos, Ava!!! Kudos. Kudos. Kudos!" says Dad, putting his arm around her flannel blanket shoulders. "You know how proud I am of you, Pumpkin."

"Kudos? What is that, Mom? It sounds like some health food cereal," says Ava, looking again like she might cry. And then she says, "These are the dresses I am making. I'll use these patterns. There are supposed to be four finished pieces for the application. I mean, I will use different fabric and everything."

"Pumpkin?" says Dad. "Um, wouldn't it be better if you, um, created your own patterns? I mean, I don't know fashion, of course, but, um, wouldn't that be better, Pumpkin? I mean, isn't that the point?"

Mom glares at Dad. "Angus, you are being critical again." Mom gets up, goes into the kitchen, rattles some pans, and doesn't come back.

"Buddy, what?" calls Dad. "I'm a Hoosier, Buddy, from Indiana, and Hoosiers are honest. I was just trying to help."

"We know you're a Hoosier, Dad," says Ava. "It's okay. I'm fine." And then she bursts into tears and stumbles back into the apartment, tripping on her blanket.

"It's almost a perfect day," says Dad. "What's with all the drama?"

"Almost perfect doesn't count," I say.

We finish breakfast, Dad and me, eating bread and butter with French jam, which tastes as if branches hung over the balcony from which we picked handfuls of fresh raspberries. But I feel uneasy and torn. Ava's red eyes, the phone ringing in the darkness last night, Logan turning in the wisteria and running.

Soon I too get up and go inside without saying much.

"Ava," I call. "Um, Logan dropped off . . . um . . ."

"Don't bother me, Pet," Ava says, disappearing down the hallway.

I turn around and look through the French doors at Dad. His shoulders are slumped a little and he sits there among the red geraniums all alone.

Chapter 29

The worry about Logan's letter has driven me forward. I have never worked so hard on a dress before. And now it is half finished. I look around the room and I get this funny feeling again. Why do I feel like someone has been in here?

I pick up my new dress. The striped sleeves are attached with pins. Some of the seams are open. I would like to sew them on a sewing machine. And so I carry my half-made dress downstairs. It looks somehow wounded on the clothes hanger, arms hanging open as if shot by Jean-Claude in some terrible battle.

Collette's door is open and I find her with her head wrapped in a big towel. She is wearing a light cotton flowered dress. "Ah, there you are!" she says. "The one my grandmother sent here."

"Oh no, Collette, your grandmother did not send me," I say. "I came here because my dad got a sabbatical."

"Oh, people often don't know when things are meant to be," Collette says. "But no worry. Today you must excuse this. I am putting the henna in my hair, as you say, to take away *le gris*, the gray!"

Collette is carrying a framed picture in her arms. She puts it on the kitchen table. It is a hand-painted photograph of a little cottage in the countryside with roses climbing up its wall.

"Oh, this is pretty. Whose house is it?" I ask.

"Oh, it's nothing," says Collette. "Just my papa's house in Provence, in the south of France."

"Is it yours now?" I ask.

"Yes, it is mine. But I never go there. Not for many years."

"Why not?" I say. "It looks so beautiful and it is not that far away."

"Oh no, no. I have things here keeping me," she says, looking away.

"Um," I say, "I have been working on this new dress." And I hold it up.

"*Mais bravo! Félicitations!* It is so much to remind me of the little one made by the Jumeau company!"

"You like the dress? What?" I say. "I mean, I wasn't sure. I thought maybe it was too weird."

"As I said before, sometimes weird is good. Did you know this?" says Collette. "Oh, but you remind me of my little Delphine Rouette. So strange, is it not? Come, let me show you how to use the treadle on the sewing machine." She tugs on my braid. "*Allons-y, ma chérie!*"

Soon I am sitting in front of the sewing machine. "Did Delphine use this machine when she worked on the doll dress?" I say as Collette shows me how to push down on the treadle with my feet. It reminds me of the pedals of a piano. It soon makes a comforting singing sound as it moves along.

"Yes," says Collette. "This is the machine she used in between handstitching. And once the doll dress was finished, as I said before, Delphine knew it was extraordinary. She was not being vain or full of ego. No, she simply saw its beauty. She hardly felt she had sewn it herself. It was as if angels had helped her make the dress!

"Of course you can imagine! She felt great excitement and also great worry. Madame Jumeau would not accept a child's work on an important dress. She would perhaps even be angry that Delphine had used Jumeau fabrics and made the dress without permission. And so Delphine did something outside of herself, outside of the rules. She thought with her own head. And for a twelve-year-old girl, she did something daring.

"When her mama was out, perhaps taking a pair of blue walking boots to be re-heeled, Delphine reached in the cupboard and took the key, which had been given to her mama for the little box in the Luxembourg Gardens. Quickly she wrapped her beautiful doll dress in paper and tucked it in a basket and she left the apartment. At first she walked, then she ran, and finally she hopped on one of those omnibuses, I think you call them, that were pulled by a team of horses. It didn't cost much to ride those omnibuses with wooden benches inside and benches up on top on the roof. And soon she got off near the Jardin du Luxembourg.

"Ah, I am sure she was nervous. I am sure she was scared. She was fragile like a tiny fairy, light on her feet, my little grandmother. Quickly she went to find the box that was tucked behind the statue near the pool of water and she unlocked the box and put the wrapped doll dress in it.

"And then she locked it back up and hurried home, knowing Madame Jumeau would go there to pick up the dress that evening, knowing Madame Jumeau would think it was created by Delphine's mama. And that is just what happened.

"Madame Jumeau collected the dress and when she took it home she loved it! She was in ecstasy over it! She hurried around her Parisian *hôtel particulier*, her private home, making plans. She loved it so much she decided immediately that it would go to the World's Fair.

"Now all the Jumeau dolls from size zero to size sixteen had their very special dresses made by the best doll couturiers in Paris. And the seventeen perfect dolls that were to go to the fair that year were ready.

"Because of the arrangement with the hiding place, the spy had not seen this last dress. And Madame announced at the workshop when all were gathered that the selections had been made. And she thanked Delphine's mama over and over again and paid her an extra bonus for the beautiful work. Delphine was at her mother's side and she tugged on her mother's arm when Madame was thanking her. Delphine tugged and tugged. Delphine's mama was confused. She looked at Delphine and frowned. She closed her eyes but she waited and didn't speak.

"Oh, things might have been different! Yes, things surely would have been different if Delphine's dress had not been so beautiful and if it had not been selected to go to the fair. But it went. Yes, it went and that size eight doll attracted all the attention! And the Jumeau doll company made a huge sensation at the fair! Everyone loved the dolls and their beautiful clothes. And most especially the size eight Bébé Jumeau and its astonishing dress. There was nothing else like that dress in the whole World's Fair and it brought home a medal for the Jumeau doll company.

"You must imagine Delphine just twelve years old. She was splitting with joy. She was singing on the rooftops. She was dancing on the bell tower of Notre-Dame Cathedral! She flew in her mind all the way to Montmartre, where all the artists lived and painted. You know, Renoir and all the others. The painter Chagall was not yet in Paris, but if he had been, he would have seen her floating by and he would have surely painted her flying over Paris.

"Delphine's mama suspected what had happened. But you know, they never spoke of it. Her mama was silent and secretly pleased and very proud. Should they tell Madame Jumeau the truth, that the beautiful dress was made by a child? Oh no, it could not be said. It was against the company rules. This was the way it was back then. You know?

"And if that had been the end of it, perhaps the rest might not have happened. Perhaps I would have been spared my sorrow. But I was not spared. No. No. Not at all."

Chapter 30

Now Collette gets up and goes out into the courtyard. She walks back and forth out there, back and forth under shadowy plane trees. Finally she returns and pats my hand and says, "Enough, Petunia, I must take Le Bon Bon out of his dark hole. I see his curtains to the courtyard are drawn. He must go with me now to buy some socks. How can someone go dancing at the Hôtel Magique without socks! No no. It is not possible."

And so I trudge back upstairs thinking about Delphine Rouette and her prizewinning doll dress. Did she ever get to say that *she* had sewn that doll dress, the one the world adored? Did she ever get to say that it was her design? Her creation?

I walk right in on Mom and Dad and Ava in the salon. They are planning to go to the Louvre museum which is open on Thursday nights. Not many people go then and that's why Dad likes it. But I do not want to wander through those rooms that are empty except for enormous paintings of horses stampeding in battle and bulls rearing up in the dust and castles deteriorating in smoke and splendor. I do not want to get lost in rooms of Napoleon's furniture, Egyptian vases, and gold-painted cupboards. Everything empty and bright and somehow desolate in the nighttime. "No, I don't want to go. I'll stay home this evening," I say.

"It's just so off the wall," says Ava, her face crinkling up with bewilderment. "Where is Logan? I am sure he would have called. Mom, have you heard from Logan?"

I look away, dropping into the pit of my being where darkness lurks and everything drips with rain. *Ginger, help me. Look into the blue mist of your yard-sale crystal ball and tell me how to change or take back what I have done!*

"Ava," I say, "um, you got a—"

Ava pushes by me, saying, "Mom, when you saw Mrs. Stewart yesterday, did she mention *anything* about Logan?"

"No, I don't think so, honey," says Mom. "We were having lunch with Nan Watson. We talked about Boston. It was nice to get out and speak English."

"Nan Watson?" I say, backing up. I start to tremble. Mom had lunch with Mrs. Stewart and Mrs. Watson?

Dad hooks an elbow around me and says, "Wish you were coming with us, sweetheart. The famous statue of Venus is at this museum. And yes, I know, she's missing a couple of arms, but then nobody's perfect." Dad kisses me on the cheek.

"Come on," Ava says. "Let's go."

"Ah yes," says Dad. "Venus, the goddess of beauty and love, awaits us at the museum. Girls, did you know Venus is also called Aphrodite? We're coming! We're on our way! All righty, Aphrodite!"

Ava reaches out to put her hand on Dad's shoulder, but he kind of changes direction in a bumbly way, not noticing, and Ava's hand falls back to her side.

Alone at home after the family leaves, I am thinking I didn't find a way to say anything to Ava. Again. And oh, I just couldn't ask about Mrs. Watson. I didn't want to know. I just hope during lunch she didn't mention to Mom anything about me and what happened at the Watson house. I would just die.

I go back into my room and stand next to the dark wooden armoire. In spite of everything, I am still wondering why someone hid that little dress in the locked drawer. Collette hasn't explained that. I open the doors of the armoire and see my two new dresses hanging in there. Mom doesn't like anything I have made here and of course Ava hates everything of mine. I am scared and I probably won't get accepted, but I am going to try to finish at least two more dresses for the fashion show application, which is due very soon.

Collette gave me a book with pictures of dolls made by the Jumeau company in the 1890s. The dolls are shown dressed in their original costumes created by Ernestine Jumeau and her team of couturiers, Delphine and her mother among them. I flip through the pages looking for a doll dress that might inspire my next design.

I finally decide on a cotton one with lace inserts and a double flounce skirt. I do happen to have some thin yellow cotton that I brought from home. America. That word is beginning to sound strange and faraway, *America*, as if I am looking through veils of yellow fabric and can barely see it. Ginger and her mom seem lost too in the bolts of blowing chiffon. And there among the waves of fabric floats another letter. The one I wrote to Windel.

After I had tried to return the overcoat and failed, Ginger said to me, "Look, you gotta contact Windel. Maybe a letter would work. This has gone on too long. Windel has to know how you feel. Tell him everything. You write it. I'll mail it. Piece of cake." We were sitting in her laundry room. She kept her crystal ball and her cards and stuff in there. She called it her office. She said the spinning dryer encouraged psychic activity. She was sitting on the dryer as she spoke. A pair of purple jeans were tossing around in there.

"Oh no!" I said. "Me? You want me to write a letter to Windel? I just don't have that kind of daring. I'm more, uh, cautious about this kind of thing," I said, pulling up my very slouching kneesocks. "A letter like that doesn't usually come from a second-born type."

"My mom says psychically you need to break free. She saw it in your stars. Let's start with the letter," Ginger said, glancing at the spinning dryer.

So I wrote the letter to Windel. And yes, it said everything. I put into it all the love I felt for him and all the joy knowing him had given me. I told him how nice it was to see him walking his brother to school every day, how sweet it was when he bought a valentine in Harvard Square, probably for his grandma because it was not long after his grandpa had died. I told him I felt bad when kids made fun of him when his music scores once fell out of his arms and blew around the lunchroom. And I told him I loved his music.

And then we mailed it. We dropped the letter in the box and it went cheerfully off on its way to the Watson residence.

But alas, I quickly grew to regret what we had done. I couldn't sleep. I tossed and turned and whined and worried. And I called Ginger every two minutes. I sent her so many emails I clogged her mailbox. Her computer crashed. Her iPhone collapsed from too many texts and way too many of my miserable selfies sent at all hours. "Ginger," I repeated over and over again, "I don't want Windel to see that letter!!!"

Finally Ginger had to break down and help me. There was only one thing to do. We had to get the letter back just after the mailman delivered it, before Windel came home from school. Good thing we didn't use email. Email moments of rashness can never be retrieved!

And so it was that Ginger and I sauntered over to Windel's street and noticed a tiny window in the Watsons' basement. It was propped open for cleaning day. Ginger poked her head through it and heard a vacuum going and we saw the cleaning lady's van parked out front. We also knew the mail had been delivered through a slot in the front door and that Windel was at the practice building where he always was at this time. Ginger took the plunge and squeezed herself through the small opening and rolled down, struggling to land on the floor of the basement. Her purple jeans got torn and dusty. I squeezed in after her. I too was covered in cobwebs.

Still we managed to creep up the stairs and open the door. We slipped into the hall. And as luck would have it, there my letter lay on the Persian carpet by the front door, all alone and waiting. Ginger grabbed it. Oh, such relief! Every time she ripped it, I felt grateful beyond measure. Grateful beyond imagining!

She stuffed the pieces of the letter in her pocket and we quickly stumbled down the basement stairs, patting each other on the back. "We did it!" Ginger whispered. "Yes!"

We were just headed for the window again when suddenly Mrs. Watson appeared in the basement with a mop in hand. She was angry. *No,* she was furious. She pulled on Ginger's sleeve. She yanked on my braid. She dragged us to the basement door. "I don't know what you two fools are up to today but Windel finds your antics unacceptable! He is *not* amused!"

She gave us both a terrible shove out the basement door. We landed on our faces in the wet, cold winter grass. "This is called breaking and entering. It's illegal.

If you stalk my son anymore, I will call the principal. I know your principal personally. I will have you expelled from school. Windel is very angry about all this! Please leave!"

Ginger and I limped away in devastation.

Of all the tangled mistakes I have made in my younger-sister life, that one was the worst. Oh, the darkness of this apartment when all the lights but mine are off! There is only the pointed beacon light shining on my sewing table.

I haven't closed my curtains yet. I look out my window and see the girl across the street. She's alone too as usual with her birds.

Everyone in Paris has a bird or a dog, it seems. Dogs are allowed to ride the city buses on leashes or sitting on laps or tucked into coat pockets. They let dogs in the restaurants too. Under many tables lurks a waiting dog, hidden mostly by the white tablecloth, though often you can see a tail sticking out. Sometimes you will see a Frenchman lean over and give half his beefsteak to something under the table. You hope it's only a dog.

The girl across from me looks rather sad, alone at night with nothing but the lights of the Paris skyline to cheer her up. Suddenly I get this Beanly idea. Grandma Beanly calls it the crazy hopping Hoosier in me. (Most of the Beanlys live in Indiana.) I get out a nice fat marker and a big piece of paper and I write in heavy letters *"Salut!"* which is a cool way to say hello in French. Because I am still part child and look like one, as Ava is quick to tell me, I can do this. I press the paper against the glass and I stand beside it. Soon she presses a piece of paper to her window that says "*Salut!*"

Then she goes back to her birds and I go back to my sketches, all the while thinking of Ava's letter from Logan. If only Ava would stop taunting me about everything. She aims and shoots so perfectly. The girl across the street has disappeared into her back rooms but she taped the word *Salut* to her window so it's still there. She appears to be so kind. I think too about Delphine and her sister. Such closeness. Oh, I wish I hadn't taken Logan's letter at all. It was wrong. Really wrong and I need to give it to Ava. Right away!

Chapter 31

The problem is, how do I go about giving Ava the letter? I decide against leaving it downstairs because it's dated four days ago and Collette is cleaning the hall and has removed the little table on which a letter might sit. I can't leave it on the floor.

Ava has been having more closed-door tête-à-tête conversations with Mom, in which I hear dangling threads like, "Honey, don't fret. I am sure he didn't kiss you and dump you. That just doesn't sound like Logan." More arrows to my heart. Ava and Logan have kissed. She gets everything. I feel so bad and lowdown I could scream.

Okay, if I hand Ava the letter, what do I say? I mean, how do I begin? And I don't want Mom to know about this. I mean, this is just between me and Ava and my own guilty conscience.

Ginger whispered to me before I left, "Anything can happen in Paris. Miraculous things!" But then Ginger isn't always right about her fortune-telling. Once she predicted Melanie was going to come home from a family trip to Vermont with a boyfriend in tow and instead she came home with a Chihuahua, one of those little dogs that bark all the time.

Miraculously an occasion finally arises for me to give Ava her letter. Mom comes out into the hall with two bags of laundry this morning. She wants Ava and me to take them to the Laundromat. "Girls," she says, "there's a sidewalk café next to the Laundromat and you two can sit outside and have a cup of something while the laundry dries. Have lunch, maybe. Here's twenty euros."

"Do I have to sit with *her*?" says Ava, wrinkling her nose at me and then putting on a pair of large sunglasses as if to block me from her sight.

"You can stand up, if you want," I say, trying to wrinkle my nose back at her. But my nose won't wrinkle. You have to have storybook skin for that.

I go in my room, feeling sure when we are sitting at the café I will find the right moment to give Ava her letter. So I zip it into my backpack and sling it over my arm. Soon Ava and I head off down the rue Michel-Ange, me the misguided elf with Santa's bag on my back and Ava swinging hers at a distance like a sleek model with a French poodle in tow.

After we load the machines in the Laundromat we go to a café and sit outside at a table along the wide stretching boulevard. There is a feeling of open sky and windy space and there is no explaining how grown-up and cool I feel suddenly having coffee with my older sister. I feel as if I am being admitted finally into the inner secret circle of grown-up older sisters and their special heavily guarded beverage, *coffee.*

Then Ava stares at my arms. "Weird. Are those cuffs on your sleeves actually made of a different fabric?" she says. "Where did you come up with that fabric, it's just bizarre."

"I found it at the Auteuil Market," I say. "I made this jacket with the leftover material from something else I made. The sleeves are cotton. The cuffs are velvet." Then I look down at my sleeves. They seem to darken in shadows suddenly.

"Something else you're making?" Ava says. "Shouldn't you be sleeping at night?"

Ava looks away, nibbling a French pastry with whipped cream inside. As I am sipping the coffee, my first real cup ever, I feel kind of extra jumpy, like a Hoosier Beanly jumping bean. I think about bringing out the letter and pause out of nervousness. Then Ava says, "There are so many empty tables out here. Why don't you sit at your own table?"

And suddenly I don't *feel* like giving her letter back to her, though I am still planning to. And then she says, "Or better yet, why don't you go put the clothes in the dryer? I'll pay the bill here."

When I was younger I was always Ava's go-to girl. *Pet, go get my jacket from the car, would you? Pet, bring me some ice cream from the fridge? Get up, Pet. I need to sit in that chair, okay?* When I was younger, did I ever question it? No. I was a dumb little kid and did all of Ava's bidding. But now that I am older, I usually refuse. But today

Logan's letter is hovering over me and so I shrug my guilt-ridden shoulders and head over to the Laundromat.

Everyone always ends up in Paris, says Ginger's mom. But you don't hear much about people doing laundry here, that's for sure. I push into the Laundromat and drag all the wet clothes into a cart and now I am standing by a dryer that looks like it might be available as soon as the apologetic man who speaks neither French nor English folds the last of his worn-out blue towels.

All the other dryers are spinning away, spinning like the earth, spinning like the stars, spinning like the great vortex that Paris seems to be, according to Ginger's mom. And it's true everyone I know, even Ava's unwanted father, is spinning toward its center. And in the jumble of it all, there is the letter from Logan, the letter that must be given to Ava as soon as I go back to the café!

So I get ready to head over there, looking around the Laundromat for my backpack. I check the table where I emptied the washers. I look on the chairs. I don't see it. Where is it? I must have left it on the counter by the dryer. No. No. Hey, what's going on? I run around the Laundromat looking under tables, even in the empty washing machines. Help!

I pound on the office door and a rumpled-looking woman appears. *"Mon sac á main,"* I say, which means "my purse." I don't know the word for backpack. "Gone," I say. "Missing! Help!"

The laundry lady looks even more rumpled and sleepy and shakes her head no. *"Non, non. Pas ici! Pas moi!"*

"It can't be gone," I say, racing around the dryers, magazines and newspapers flying at my touch.

Soon Ava leans in the door of the Laundromat and calls out in her usual grumpy way, "Pet, what *are* you doing? You're always soooo slow. I am heading home now. Fold everything so it will fit in one bag, okay?"

"But wait! I lost my backpack. It's gone," I say. "Someone must have taken it."

"Maybe you left it at the apartment or something. I'll let you know if I see it," she says.

"But, Ava, wait!" I call out. Ava has always been a quick leaver. When she wants to go, she's gone. And now she hurries off at an I-couldn't-care-less older-sister gallop.

And I am left standing in the Laundromat, knowing Ava's love letter from Logan has been stolen along with my backpack. I stand in the middle of Paris alone, in the center of the spinning vortex.

Chapter 32

Now I am in a pickle, to use a Grandma Beanly phrase. No, it's worse than that. I should say, now I *feel* like a big, green, stupid pickle on legs. Some robber has Logan's letter. His secret heart is being tossed about, maybe even mocked by some stranger. Why was I such an idiot? Why did I take what was not mine? Now I will have to confront Ava and explain. And this may be outside my capabilities.

Then it occurs to me that I could tell Logan his letter was lost, that the concierge threw it away by mistake and then told me. "So, um, Logan, you may have to write another letter to Ava," I imagine myself saying.

When I get home I am full of resolve. I will be a better younger sister. To make up for what I have done, I will rewrite that book. It will still be called, as I planned, *How to Be a Younger Sister.* But it will include mostly instructions on becoming a selfless server, admiring, unassuming, helpful.

I go over to my sewing table and gather up the yellow cotton fabric, all cut out and ready to sew. This time I just ignore that things look moved around. I decide I have an American case of paranoia due to extreme culture shock.

I gather up the fabric and carry it down to Collette's apartment. When I lay all the cutout pieces on her table, the dress looks like something fragmented and broken, something that needs putting back together, gluing, repairing, like me right now, like Collette right now, like Ava right now, like Mom right now, like Le Bon Bon right now. The only person it doesn't remind me of is Dad. Dad is already in one good solid piece. And yet we're all here because of him and his sabbatical.

I try to explain to Collette about Logan's letter but of course it doesn't come out quite right when I actually put it in words. I end by saying, "So can I tell Logan you threw it out by mistake?"

"Well, yes, you can do that. But perhaps it is not so good to lie. This is when the tangles get tighter," says Collette. "This is like Le Bon Bon. He tries to tell me he is fine, that he likes to live in the darkness with the curtains closed, that he doesn't want another love. But of course he is lying to himself and to me."

"I know," I say. "He's very sad."

"There will be a dance for families this week in the lobby at the Hôtel Magique. Anyone can go and dance *le swing*. I will take Le Bon Bon and Jean-Claude and *peut-être* you will come too? You can dance with Jean-Claude."

"I don't know how to dance *le swing*," I say.

"Oh, it's 1950s and early 1960s, you know, Johnny Hallyday and the big guitar. With the beat it will be natural. You will see. Jean-Claude and Le Bon Bon are both good dancers."

"Jean-Claude can dance *le swing*?" I say.

"Oh, *mais oui! Oui!* He learned when he was four years old," says Collette. "His uncle taught him. Okay? I will say to your friend that I am so sorry I threw out the letter, if you will go with us. We need someone for Jean-Claude to dance with. You are both children."

"Okay," I say. "But I am not a child."

"You are *a halfway*, like Delphine Rouette, half in one world, half in the other," says Collette, smiling at me.

And then I show Collette the doll dress in the Jumeau book that has inspired my next design and I show her my sketches.

"Oui," she says when she sees the picture in the book. "This dress was created at the height of Jumeau, when the company was thriving. But I told you before there was trouble. Those who attended the World's Fair in Chicago could see it. Amid all of the attention and acclaim for the little size-eight doll and her doll dress, those who knew saw what was wrong.

"In the toy pavilion you could see many of the German doll dresses and styles mirrored the Jumeau dresses. Some would say the word *copied*. They looked quite like them, and these dresses and dolls were cheaper. Much cheaper. I told you that spies had managed to steal the ideas for many of the dresses that came out of the workshop of Madame Jumeau. Ah, but not Delphine Rouette's dress.

No one had seen that one until it arrived at the fair. Thus, it was unique.

"You can imagine the sadness for Madame Ernestine Jumeau and the disappointment, knowing someone among her workers was spying, taking her ideas, sketching them, and selling those sketches to a German doll company.

"Madame Jumeau was sure now that the time had come to do something about it. In her great dismay, she went to visit Delphine Rouette's mama.

"It was a miracle to have such an important and celebrated lady in their apartment. They served tea and cakes and sat just over here by the window. Yes, in this very salon. My grandmother told me about it. She remarked that Madame Jumeau wore a pale rose silk walking suit and carried a rose-tinted parasol.

" 'I need your help,' said Ernestine Jumeau, sipping her tea. 'I need you and your little daughter to be my eyes and my ears. You have worked for me for so long. I can trust you. We must find out who among us is selling my designs to Handwerck, to Kestner, and to the others. The German doll companies are trying to bring down the House of Jumeau.

" 'But I have made a plan,' she said. 'I will change our hiding place. From now on you will leave the doll dresses and the slips you make in the basement of l'église de la Madeleine. The church of the Madeleine. The great church near la place Vendôme. I know the priest there.

He will help us. I will let it circulate at my workshop that we are using the Luxembourg Gardens as a hiding place and I will leave the key to the box hanging in plain sight at my workshop. But we will not use that hiding place anymore. No. Instead I will leave a doll dress in that box as a lure, a decoy. Then you and your daughter can watch and wait and see who goes there to make drawings of it.'

"And so it was. Every day, every week thereafter, Delphine and her mama would take a stroll in the Luxembourg Gardens and they would picnic by the pool and walk past the statues. But they saw nothing. The spy did not appear and the whole month passed and nothing odd turned up.

"Finally one evening Delphine had gone with her mother to the puppet show in the park. Though she was twelve, Delphine still had her rag doll sitting on her bed at home that her mama had made for her. Oh, that doll meant so much to Delphine. Her name was Chiffons, or Rags in English. She was only a cloth doll.

"Delphine never had a fancy doll with a porcelain head, the kind Jumeau made. They were too expensive. But she saw many lucky children in the Luxembourg Gardens with their beautiful Jumeau dolls dressed sometimes in outfits created by Delphine's mama. Oh, but the world is never fair or just, is it? And back in those days, this is how things were.

"That day Delphine's mama had an appointment not far off and she left Delphine watching the puppet show in the Luxembourg Gardens. Soon the show was over and Delphine wandered a little toward the pool where the cupid leaned into the water. She was sitting in the shade near some tulips when she spotted a figure in a dark skirt and jacket going toward the pool.

"Delphine moved closer and slipped into the bushes to hide. Oh *mon Dieu*! *Mon Dieu!* What Delphine saw! It was the spy. The spy had come to the box behind the statue.

"Delphine crept even nearer down among the leaves. It was hard to see in the shade and the shadows. The closer she got, the more sure she was. The more sure she was, the more her heart fell, the more it dropped, like a bird shot dead.

"Now she could see who the spy was. And who was it? It was Sylvie! Her dear sister! Sylvie was sitting in the shadows quickly sketching the dress. Oh *mon Dieu*! Oh, angels in heaven! Oh, sky above. Oh, clouds. Oh, rain. Oh, wind! Say it's not so! Sylvie, who rubbed her feet and sponged her forehead when Delphine once had a high fever. Sylvie. She had grown up with her. They shared everything. She wrote her letters every day! Sylvie was the closest person in the world to her. She knew Sylvie's every breath. For all their lives their rag dolls had been best friends. She loved Sylvie!

"Delphine did not wait for her mama. She ran all the way from the Luxembourg Gardens, rushing across Paris, passing the brand-new Eiffel Tower and then on into Passy. She ran until her lungs hurt and her eyes hurt. 'No no no,' she kept crying. 'Say it's not so.' But it was so. It was so! Sylvie, her dearest, beloved stepsister, was the spy.

"Delphine felt like thin cotton torn in two pieces, she felt ripped like a length of linen, shredded like a yard of silk. But by the time she got home, exhausted, hungry, and wet from the rain, she knew. She knew she could never tell on her sister. Sylvie was poor. Her papa was out of work. Delphine could never say what she saw. She told no one, not even her mama."

Collette's voice is quavering now. Her words are hushed and breathy. Her head is bent and her hands are twisted around each other, knotted together. "What would you have done, Petunia? If your sister was the spy? Someone who was so close to you they could almost feel your thoughts? Someone you loved so very much. Where would *your* loyalties have been?"

Chapter 33

Mom and Ava have gone out to get shampoos and manicures and then they are going to have dinner at a restaurant called Bonjour Paris! Dad said before they left, "It sounds like a tourist trap, Buddy. If you want the real French experience, go to the Café de Flore. That's where all the cool French people eat."

But Mom and Ava are sure that's where they want to go, even though Bonjour Paris! didn't even get mentioned in Rick Steves' guide. They left a couple of hours ago. Now Dad is in his study working on an article about Flaubert (who else?).

I feel sad and sorry for Delphine Rouette. She was caught in a trap, not wanting to betray her sister and not wanting to hurt the Jumeau company. What was she to do? Some things don't seem to have answers. I am caught in a trap too. But it is a trap my own stupidity caused. I never thought someone would steal my backpack.

I lean in through Dad's doorway. He's at his desk with piles of books all around him. He looks up and says, "Flaubert hated modern life in the 1860s. You know that, Pet? He refused to ride the train to Paris. He took instead a boat down the Seine from his house. He liked the old-fashioned life. And he was right!" Dad pounds his fist down on his desk. "Progress will destroy us."

"Dad, Mom says to be careful with the Barbours' furniture," I say.

"Thank heavens the French like their trains," says Dad. "In the States the trains have all but disappeared." He sticks his head back behind his book and I go off to my room, feeling alone with my secret and wondering how Delphine Rouette felt with hers.

It's dusk and Paris is a dark gray pearl with orange lanterns of light in all its many windows. I can see that the young woman across the street is in her salon, as usual. For the first time I see this evening she has a visitor, a man wearing a white doctor's jacket with a stethoscope around his neck.

Now he holds a little finch in his hands, putting the stethoscope against its chest. When he tucks the bird back in the cage, he stands up and looks at the girl. Then he starts gesturing with his right hand rapidly, as if talking with his hands. She in turn responds with her hand moving quickly, fingers to the side and then straight up, then hand closed. Then open.

Soon the girl walks the man to the door and they disappear. After a few minutes I see him on the sidewalk below passing under a streetlamp, carrying a doctor's bag. I decide he must be a veterinarian. Either he is a friend or veterinarians make house calls in Paris.

I turn now to my yellow cotton dress. Collette showed me how to make French seams so that the inside of the dress does not look all ragged and as if it might unravel. She also gave me a cardboard of old narrow lace to use for the inserts in the front of the bodice. Tomorrow I will try to reach Logan, though I am not sure how to tell him. I don't even know how to find his phone number in Paris. I will also go back to the Laundromat to see if my backpack has turned up. I feel a great sadness creeping over me. Not just *my* sadness, but Delphine Rouette's sadness. Hers seemed to be unfixable.

I look over and see the young woman across the street is back in her salon now. She leans near her birdcage with a worried look on her face. I feel worried too. We seem to mirror each other, she and I, like sisters. I get my markers out and write in bold letters, *Salut! Je m'appelle Petunia. Je suis américaine,* which means "Hello. My name is Petunia. I am American."

She soon sees my note and writes back, *Salut. Je m'appelle Marguerite. Je suis sourde.* Her name is Marguerite. We wave and smile and then Marguerite goes back to her birds, filling the water dispenser on the cage.

I do not know what *Je suis sourde* means and so I go down the smaller hall that leads to the little toilette behind its door, and then to Mom and Dad's bedroom and finally to Dad's study. I lean in the doorway where

Dad sits among his towers of books. "Dad," I say, "what does *Je suis sourde* mean?"

Dad looks at me, pleasant and puzzled in a Dad kind of way. He puts his book down and says, "Honey, it means 'I am deaf.' "

"Oh, thanks," I say and then I go back down the hall and find my way to the kitchen. I sit down. In the center of the table, there is a bowl of blood oranges. Even the fruit is slightly different here. Nothing is entirely familiar. Nothing. I put my head down on the table and for the first time since I have been in Paris, I cry.

Chapter 34

Today I hear Mom on her phone talking to Mrs. Stewart. By stitching the threads of their conversation together, I figure out that Logan is away traveling in the north of France with his dad. Heartbroken and rejected, he must have taken off into the wilds, to be alone, to think, to brood. Naturally this upsets me further.

I feel so bad that I even go into Ava's room and fumble around trying to explain, mumbling phrases like "stolen letter" and "missing backpack" but my words get all snarled up and make no sense. Ava looks amused and superior and so I slink away sorrowfully. When I was in her room I did notice that she covered something up quickly with her bedspread and pushed something behind her so I couldn't see whatever it was. But that's Ava for you.

I go back to my room for my sparkly silver sweater that I got while in New York City just before we left our home, America. That sweater is one of the only things I own that Ava wants. She once asked me to trade for the sweater. She offered me a pair of socks with a button on them that plays "We Wish You a Merry Christmas." But I declined.

Now I put the sparkly silver sweater on her bed and say, "It's yours, Ava. I have decided it's not my color." Ava looks pleased, as if it's her natural right, and puts it on immediately over her nightgown. Then she flops down on the chaise lounge in the corner and begins reading, wearing *my* favorite silver sweater. And still I feel dreadful. Awful. Terrible.

A little later, I decide to make lunch for Ava, bread, cheese, and fresh sliced tomato. On the tray I include my new jar of Nutella, which is a nutty chocolate spread French kids eat on everything. It is now Ava's favorite food in France (mine too). I bought the jar with the last drop of Grandma Beanly's "bon voyage" money. I was saving the delightful treat for my own late-night emergencies.

I take the tray into Ava's room and set it on her desk. She looks up briefly from her book and nods, as if to say, "Very good, Wilson, that will be all." When I come back to get the tray I see she has eaten the whole jar of *my* Nutella and nothing else. And still I don't complain.

Later Ava calls out, "Pet, my sunglasses are missing. Find them for me, will ya?" And I go galloping, in my shame and guilt, around the apartment, climbing under tables and squeezing into tight spaces where sunglasses might wander. Finally I find them in the bottom of the standing water in the bathtub. (The tub water takes about two hours to drain. I timed it once.) Well, at least the sunglasses were not in *la toilette.*

Alas, I realized as I reached into the tepid bathwater, I can never actually tell Ava what happened with the letter. If she knew, she might truly kill me. Mom would too. They would have to bury me beneath the Statue of Liberty that stands along the river not far from here. It is the smaller, unimportant, younger sister of the real Statue of Liberty in New York City. A perfect resting spot for me. And then, of course, I would never make it back to my beloved U.S. of A.

Today Ava brought home a cute stray puppy that was running lost through the Parc du Ranelagh and she spent hours calling the phone number on the collar. Just now she has located the grateful owner, who is on his way over here.

Yes, Ava can be sweet at times. I remember how she trained all the dogs in Grandma Beanly's neighborhood in Indiana one summer. She taught them to sit up and beg and do all kinds of tricks. Then I helped her put on a dog circus for everyone. It was so much fun. Oh, I wish I had never stolen Ava's letter.

Still, through all this, I have managed to complete the yellow dress and one more, the final one. Now I have four finished.

Collette has helped me fill out the application for the fashion show on her computer using her email address. I borrowed Monsieur Le Bon Bon's digital camera and I took the photos. I wrote an essay to go with them and then we pushed the send button and the application went off into the unknown to be weighed and criticized by unseen judges. Ever since we sent off the application by email, my whole being has been rattled. Why did I even want to try?

And I feel so rotten about ruining Ava's love life that I am thinking maybe I should go downstairs and wither away under the wisteria.

When I get downstairs, the first thing I say is, "Collette, have we heard from the fashion show people yet?"

"So soon, *ma petite*? No. No. This takes time," Collette says. She is carrying a big angry bumblebee out of her kitchen. She has him caught in a jar and he is fighting the glass wall.

I am standing here wondering, how much time will it take before we hear about the show? Will I be jittery like this for a whole month?

"Non, non, monsieur!" says Collette to the bumblebee. "Stop buzzing. You cannot break the glass. It is not possible. You must allow me to help you, monsieur." She carries the jar to the courtyard and I follow. Then she opens the lid and lets the fussing, buzzing bee out. He soars angrily off toward the sky. *"Voilà!"* she says. "Go home now, monsieur, back to your hive. The flowers in the courtyard at the school for the deaf attract all the bees in Paris. That is where this bee was going, I am sure. The bees from that school are always coming in my kitchen!" She pats the table. "*Voilà!* Sit down, my little angel."

I droop into the chair and tuck my head down. "Ah, I see," says Collette, "things have gotten more tangled upstairs. You have not given Logan the message that the neglectful concierge has thrown away his letter! But in spite of this, I hope you will still accompany us. We are all ready to go to the Hôtel Magique this very afternoon. Monsieur Le Bon Bon is having his bath right now. Jean-Claude will arrive in one hour. As I showed you yesterday, I have the skirt from the 1950s with the Eiffel Tower on it for you to wear. It is so pretty, is it not?"

"Yes, it is. And I will be happy to wear it. I worked on these shoes to match it. I added the velvet and the stuff on the toes," I say, showing her the shoes.

"Oh, I like the red velvet and the little mouse on each toe sitting up to beg. *Elles sont adorables!*" says Collette.

"Well, they aren't mice actually. They're supposed to be French poodles. When Ava saw these shoes she said they gave her the creeps. She hates mice," I say.

"Ah, *oui*, everything gives Ava the creeps," says Collette. "What's wrong with mice? They are *très mignonnes*, very cute!"

"If it's anything to do with me, it creeps Ava," I say. "And things are a mess anyway because of me. And I wish I hadn't applied for that fashion show. If I don't get in, I am going to feel even worse."

"Well, we cannot expect to succeed at everything. Sometimes we fall down. Then we get up again. *Oui?* Oh yes, of course you're worried. How you remind me always of my little Delphine Rouette. Indeed things were a mess for her as well."

"Yes," I say. "They were."

"Well, you know her dearest sister, because of poverty and need, had betrayed the Jumeau company. And Delphine and her mama loved and needed the Jumeau company. But my little Delphine could do nothing with what she knew about Sylvie. She was caught. Trapped between two loyalties. And does anything come before family and a beloved sister?"

"Um," I say, kind of chewing on my lower lip.

"All Delphine could do to make matters better was to help Madame Jumeau as much as she could. And so she did. She sewed piles and piles of slips and bloomers for dolls and then did not record her hours and asked for no money for the work. Every time she could manage she would secretly sew a lovely doll dress and add it in with her mother's package at no charge. Whenever she could, she would go to the workshop and sweep and clean and arrange fabrics and unscramble spools of ribbon. If they needed a child to sew buttons on doll dresses or hem skirts, she would offer and then forget to write her hours down. Anything she could think of she did to help Madame Jumeau and her doll company. And Madame was very grateful to Delphine and her mama. They were her dearest and best employees.

"One day outside the house, yes on this rue Michel-Ange, two horses pulling a Jumeau doll company wagon stopped in front of the door here. And Madame Jumeau got out, carrying a box. She came into the foyer and she set the box on a small table. Then she threw her arms around Delphine's mama. 'Oh, I am so grateful for your wonderful service to the company, for the doll dress you made that won the prize. I am also grateful for your daughter's help with the slips and pantaloons. I have come to give you a gift.

" 'First I must explain that my husband and I have decided something. The Jumeau doll company will be closing its doors soon. The German doll companies have driven the price of dolls down so low that we cannot make any money. Our dolls and doll clothes take time and artistry to create. The German dolls are made quickly. They are lighter and coarser. But they are also much cheaper. We are losing money now. We must close the company.' Madame began to cry and Delphine's mama began to cry and Delphine too cried. In fact, Delphine's tears fell the hardest and the longest, for she had extra sorrow because of Sylvie.

" 'But I will never forget your service and help,' said Madame Jumeau. 'I will never forget the exquisite orange-and-maroon doll dress you made that won the medal at the World's Fair in America a few years ago.' She hugged Delphine's mama again. 'I have a very special present for you and your wonderful daughter. There are sixteen more boxes in the carriage and I will need help carrying them all in. Do you know what is inside them? Can you guess?' said Madame Jumeau."

Collette stops talking now. She turns her head and looks out at the courtyard. "And you, Petunia, do you know what Madame Jumeau gave Delphine's mama and Delphine?"

"No," I say.

"Can you remember how many Jumeau dolls went to the World's Fair in Chicago?"

"Seventeen dolls," I say. "Size zero doll, size one doll, all the way up to size sixteen."

"That's right," says Collette. "Madame Jumeau gave them all seventeen dolls dressed in the finest doll clothes, the very dolls that had gone to the fair and won the medal for the Jumeau doll company. These child dolls Madame Jumeau brought into the apartment and gave to Delphine and her mama.

"And it might have been a wonderful gift. It *should* have been. Imagine how dazzling it was for Delphine, who only owned her little doll Rags before this. Now she had seventeen of the world's most expensive and beautiful dolls. Oh, how things might have been different for me if Madame had not bestowed such a gift on my small grandmother! But she did. Oh yes, she did and what was to follow would change the course of my life as well."

Chapter 35

A small, dark cowboy rushes into Collette's kitchen and jumps into her arms. He kisses her on both cheeks. He is wearing a black Lone Ranger mask and a black cowboy shirt and black boots and a white cowboy hat. "Collette, I am all ready and set to go to dance *le swing*," Jean-Claude calls out. "I am ready to dance at the Hôtel Magique! My uncle too is all clean but his hair is wet."

"Le Bon Bon's hair will dry as he walks along the street. He cannot use that as an excuse. *C'est une excuse!* Is he hiding?" says Collette. "Do you see what Petunia is wearing? And look, she has made little shoes to match!"

"I like the mice," says Jean-Claude. "May I shoot them?"

"No shooting this afternoon, please," I say. "And those are poodles, not mice."

"It's a fake gun, just my hand, you see?" Jean-Claude pulls the mask from his eyes. "And also, it's *me,* Mademoiselle Petunia! I am here for a kiss!"

"Some other time, Jean-Claude. But I must say, your English is very good. I do not think you need me to teach you much," I say.

"Allons-y, mes amis," says Collette. "Let's go."

Collette and I troop out into the hall. Behind us, the Lone Ranger darts from corner to corner. We open Monsieur Le Bon Bon's door and Collette calls out, "*Mon petit chou!* Where are you?"

She stops for a moment in his salon, looking at the empty wall above Monsieur Le Bon Bon's sofa. "You see this large space? It's like a hole in his apartment. There used to be a painting here of Le Bon Bon's wife. It was a portrait of *her*. Le Bon Bon adored that painting. He showed it to me many times. But when *she* left, she took the painting with her! *Incroyable!* Unbelievable! She takes it with her, leaving a big hole in Le Bon Bon's heart and also a hole right here." She slaps the wall.

"It's too bad," I say.

"Perhaps he needs another painting," Collette says, whispering to herself. Then she calls out, "Le Bon Bon? Where are you? You are not trying to get out of this. We are going now."

Finally Monsieur emerges from a small room with a towel over his shoulders. He is also wearing his new silk shirt and a bow tie sewn by Collette. Every one of us is now in costume, even Collette. She is wearing a little black straw hat with a veil and white gloves that she used in the 1950s.

"No, no, you don't need this towel. Okay?" says Collette, removing the towel and tossing it aside.

Soon we all walk outside under the wisteria. The perfume of it drifts over me, as if it is some kind of magic potion, making me forget my worries. I hear the nightingale that lives in the wisteria calling now and for the first time I catch a glimpse of it as it rises above the trees.

We walk along the rue Michel-Ange, the street called Michael the angel. The perfume of the wisteria is heady and lush, the sunlight dusky, the afternoon asleep in its shimmering heat.

We cross the street and pass the building just opposite ours, and coming down the steps, I see Marguerite! All this time Marguerite has always been up high in the world of the "first floor," as the French call it, or the world of the "second floor," as Americans call it. Marguerite has always been as if floating, never on the ground, always at night when lamps are on. She was like a nighttime mirage until now.

"Marguerite!" I call out and wave. I do not think she can hear me call her name, but she can see me waving, jumping up and down. Perhaps we look funny to her, a troop of clowns dressed in costume headed for a dance. "This is Marguerite!" I say. She smiles and I smile. I try to introduce everyone. I wave and shake my head yes.

Soon Collette looks at me. "Perhaps Marguerite would like to come with us," she says. Collette then begins to speak with her hands and Marguerite begins to answer with her hands. They talk and talk with their hands in different positions, their fingers leaping and twirling. Marguerite laughs. Collette laughs. Monsieur Le Bon Bon and Jean-Claude and I stand perfectly still waiting.

Finally Jean-Claude breaks down and shoots Marguerite in the arm. "Bam Bam," he goes. Marguerite pretends to faint and holds her arm as if wounded. She fakes tears and dismay. Everybody laughs and suddenly Jean-Claude has a new friend.

Collette takes from her purse another pair of gloves and a 1950s silk scarf. She gives the scarf and gloves to Marguerite. Then Collette pats her on the back and we all meander along together down the rue Michel-Ange, headed for the Hôtel Magique.

"Marguerite takes care of the birds at the school for the deaf around the corner. I myself worked there as a concierge on weekends years ago," says Collette.

We walk six blocks, passing flower shops and restaurants with tables on the sidewalk where everyone seems to be eating and celebrating, or preparing to celebrate, emerging from the flower shops carrying bouquets.

The Hôtel Magique (Americans call it the Hotel Magic) is just off Avenue Mozart on a funny little twisted side street. It is not a grand hotel. It is small and neat with another trellis of wisteria climbing up the front. A poster standing in a frame outside announces in French, *Dansez le swing ici cet après-midi!* I hear jazzy music bubbling from the entrance. Collette puts her arm around Monsieur Le Bon Bon. Then she says, "*Bon courage*, Le Bon Bon! You know, Petunia, he shines when he dances. You'll see!"

"You are going to dance with little mice on your toes," says Jean-Claude.

“I told you, those are poodles, Jean-Claude,” I say.

“I will like to dance with the little mice,” he says. “I am a good dancer.”

“I am not,” I say. “I think I will just watch. Marguerite and I will eat crackers.”

The music when we walk in is dreamy and wraps around everything like moving water. A piano and saxophone are intertwining notes. A man stands near a microphone playing the saxophone, ribbons of sound spilling from its body. The notes of the piano behind tumble down a quick scale, then climb back up in puffs of rhythm. The smell of wisteria, the tiny glowing lights like stars along the ceiling, everybody dancing, even me. Jean-Claude is twirling me around, the room is spinning. I see Collette dancing too with Monsieur Le Bon Bon. He turns like silk, slipping in and out of twirls, winding in and out and around the music. He is the one everyone watches with his dazzling leaps and his clever jumps.

Then I spin around again and more people are dancing. And suddenly I see something wonderful. Collette has brought Marguerite to the floor. Now Monsieur Le Bon Bon and Marguerite are dancing together. They are dancing in perfect unison. Even though she is deaf, she told Collette she likes to feel the floor shake with the rhythm. Marguerite and Le Bon Bon seem suddenly to be wrapping in and out and around each other and smiling.

Collette sees it too from across the room and her face is steeped in a warm beam of extra light. The room is a beautiful wisteria blur, all lit up and joyous, even though I am dancing with the Lone Ranger, who is four years younger and four years shorter than me.

Then the musicians wish to take a break. The saxophone player announces it. *"Bonjour,"* he says. *"Merci!"* He makes a few jokes. Collette translates for me. Then he goes on to say in French that he would like to introduce us to the piano player, who happens to be staying here in the hotel. "He's here by chance, by luck, because he will be playing an important event at the Salle Pleyel coming up. He is very young. Give him a hand! Here's Windel Watson."

The crowd cheers and I fall back against the wall, my head spinning. I start choking. There Windel stands on the little stage. He is wearing his grandfather's tuxedo again and the red high-top sneakers. He gives a tilted smile to the audience. His bow tie is a little crooked, his sleeves a little long. *"Merci beaucoup!"* he says, looking up at the ceiling. Then his eyes roam around the room and they land on me. He seems to jolt backward, almost knocking over the microphone. He looks at me with his dark, brooding, startled piano eyes. "Windel is not amused!" his mother had shouted at us. "He is *very* angry!"

Suddenly the beautiful room collapses around me. Everything goes dark and begins to spin, faces fly past me, hands and arms tangle around me and I push them away trying to scramble through the maze, the thicket of legs and feet and darkness and noise. I scramble and squirm and I squeeze my way to the door to the edge of the Hôtel Magique, and I plunge out into the daylight and I start running and running and running.

Chapter 36

How long I run I cannot say. Where I end up I do not know. When I finally find a bench, I collapse on it, still crying and sniffling and sneezing. I look down at myself and see I have been through water and greenery because there are wet leaves on my skirt, mud on my knees, and I am missing a shoe. I know Ginger's mom always says Paris is a spinning vortex, the center of the world where everyone ends up, but I had hoped when I crossed the ocean I could truly close that awful chapter of my so-far-embarrassing life. How could Windel have crept through the cracks in my escape plans? Why did he have to suddenly turn up at the Hotel Magic? *Dominoes collapsing, a chain reaction, never ending.*

I go back to my tears and let them fall where they will, but when I look up I see Collette in her veiled hat holding the little hand of the Lone Ranger crossing the street, followed by Monsieur Le Bon Bon and Marguerite. They all come up around me and look sadly at me. "*Ma chérie*," says Collette, "what is the matter? What has happened and where is your shoe?"

"I don't know," I say.

"Mademoiselle was not having fun?" says Jean-Claude.

"No, no, I was. I was. I *was* having fun . . . until . . . never mind," I say.

"They will go home now," says Collette, nodding at Marguerite. "I will sit with you on your bench." She gestures to Monsieur Le Bon Bon, shooing him away gently.

Soon she waves to Jean-Claude and Le Bon Bon and Marguerite as they walk off down the street. Marguerite holds Jean-Claude's hand on one side and Monsieur Le Bon Bon holds his other hand on the other side.

"Hmmm," says Collette as they walk under a shady tree, "they look almost like a little family, do they not?"

"Yes, they do," I say.

"Now," she says, "what happened?"

"Windel Watson," I say.

"*Ah*, *oui*, the boy who plays the piano. He is very handsome. He looks like Jim Morrison from the band The Doors except for the glasses."

"Who is that?" I say.

"Oh, a band when I was younger, a long, long time ago. The Doors. *Très beau*," she says. "Your friend is very handsome. But the glasses do not suit him at all."

"He wasn't before. He didn't used to be," I say.

"He wasn't handsome until you loved him?" she says.

"That's right," I say.

"Ah, I see, this one does not belong to your older sister?"

"No," I say.

"Well, that's good! You should be happy he came to Paris."

"No, no, he hates me. His mother hates me."

"I see. But why?"

"Well, because, I am sorry to say, I stalked him. I mean, I lost his overcoat and I ruined a Valentine's party for his brother, and *other* things."

"*Other* things?"

"Umm, yes."

"Ah, Petunia, in your America you have created another tangled mess?"

"Yes, I am afraid so," I say. "And then there is the problem with Logan and the letter and Ava and her other father. And my mom is not happy in France and . . ."

"Oh, I see. You know, I am thinking that I need to give Le Bon Bon a going-away present."

"Who is going away?" I ask.

"I don't know but I think a going-away present would be nice. Don't you? I need to buy a painting for him. I think a painting of his parrot, Albert, would be perfect in that empty spot, don't you? I would like to pay your mama to make a painting of Albert. Do you think she would do it?" says Collette.

"If you ask, perhaps. She would like a job, I know," I say.

"She needs to be happy with herself," says Collette. "When a mama is happy, everyone is happy. I hope she will do it. Now, do you think you can walk home with only one shoe?"

Chapter 37

Collette and I do not get up right away. We just sit there on the bench. Collette reaches in her pocket and scatters bread crumbs on the sidewalk before us. "Oh, the sparrows of Paris so brown and plain, nobody thinks of them. But they are always there when you feel sad. They are always ready to sing a little song to cheer you up, *n'est-ce pas*? Have you been to the train station they call the Gare du Nord?"

"Yes, when we first came here," I say. "My dad was so excited to see it."

"Well, you can't sit at a table there without a little brown sparrow sitting down with you. They live inside the train station! I always bring some crumbs for the sparrows wherever I go. Paris has not changed so much in all these years. It has been like this since Degas roamed these streets. In Montmartre, Matisse the painter used to try to trade one of his early paintings for a cheese sandwich at a café. But the patron, the owner, turned him down. I knew that owner when I was young. He used to tell me he was still kicking himself about that because the paintings of Matisse now sell for millions of euros. But we all make mistakes."

"I know," I say. "But I seem to make more than my share."

"I too have made my mistakes. I tell myself I must be like silk in the wind, you know, forgiving, accepting, flexible. For me it is harder. My mistake was much graver. More terrible."

"What was your mistake, Collette?" I ask.

"Ahhh, I have told no one. Not a soul. My mistake lives alone in the darkness within me," she says.

"Dad says I am a good listener."

"Your papa is charming! Of course you are a good listener! You are *mon petit ange*, my little angel."

"Angels don't steal letters, Collette," I say.

"Oh, sometimes they do. Perhaps something good will come of it. You will see!" she says.

"What was your mistake, Collette?" I ask again.

"So easy the question. So hard the answer," she says.

"Please, Collette, I have told you so much. You can tell me. I will keep it a secret. I promise," I say.

"Secrets are not good things, my little angel," she says. "You know that and I know that. Let us walk home together now. But we will be careful of the glass on the sidewalk because you only have one shoe. And such shoes they are! I have never seen a little girl with two mice sitting on the ends of her toes. It is a shame you lost one of them."

"They are supposed to be poodles," I say again.

"To own seventeen beautiful dolls," says Collette, quietly facing forward as if she has finally decided on something. She takes my hand now and squeezes it. "Such joy and such sorrow for little Delphine, because in her heart she felt as if she had been the reason the Jumeau doll company closed its doors. How she agonized and regretted. And so the dolls in their great beauty were covered in shadows.

"Delphine thus grew up in a kind of half-hidden way. Secrets left in the dark, you know, become so very heavy. Imagine how heavy Delphine's secret must have been all that time.

"Over the years something had changed between Delphine and her sister because of it. Distance had grown between them. Perhaps because they never talked about the things that had happened. Then Sylvie was married and went away with her husband to America. Delphine never saw her sister again.

"It was too bad," says Collette. "And I know that my grandmother was deeply saddened by the loss.

"And time passed in Paris. It passed with the turning trees and the moving sky just as it does now, and one day Delphine herself was married and finally she had a child. Through all that time in her sadness, Delphine kept the dolls safely. Since she had a complete set of them, a rarity indeed, soon people began to hear of the collection and would ask to see them. After all, Delphine had worked with the famous Madame Jumeau. Still, all through the

1920s and 1930s the dolls sat quietly on shelves. And other people began to collect Jumeau dolls and their prices soared."

"Like the paintings of Matisse?" I say.

"Yes, a little," says Collette. "These dolls were part of the history of France and part of her great heritage. This is what these dolls meant to Delphine Rouette. And then came the 1940s and World War II. The Nazis invaded Paris.

"I was a little girl, and I adored my grandmother, Delphine. She was so little and fragile and quick. *Elle était toute petite! Toute petite!* She never grew very tall. I spent all my time with her and wanted to be like her. She lived upstairs in those days in the apartment where you live now.

"Ah, but we were in the midst of a war and we tried to live quietly, to manage with food shortages and the cold. But sadly the Nazis were here in Paris to take everything they could from France. They planned to take all the art, all the beautiful furniture and objects and send them to Germany for themselves. You see, the Germans and the French have never gotten along.

"The Nazi officers too had heard of my grandmother's doll collection given to her by Madame Ernestine Jumeau. And they wanted those dolls for Germany, which they called their fatherland. Oh yes, they did.

"One day my grandmother received a letter. I can remember the very morning. Her face was suddenly the color of a changing sky, dark, the way it looks after a bomber has crossed overhead. And we saw plenty of those. Oh yes, we did. In the official letter my grandmother was asked to come to the Nazi Headquarters situated in Paris. Imagine, those headquarters were now in the Luxembourg Palace. Nazi soldiers now stood in the gardens by the pool.

"Of course she did not go. She was her own person, was she not, little Delphine Rouette? Her husband, my grandfather, had died a few years before the war and no one could tell her now what to do or where to go. She simply refused. She had once let down the Jumeau doll company and she had suffered for it for many years. But she was not going to do so now.

" 'No,' she told me, 'these dolls are a national treasure of France. These dolls *are* France at her best and most glorious. And this time the Germans will not steal them. This time I will stand firm. I will not relent. They cannot have them.' My grandmother then proceeded to hide all seventeen dolls. I helped her. We worked together.

"I was a child and anything my grandmother told me I listened to and believed. I obeyed her, of course. It was the natural thing. I did not even think about disobeying. Another letter arrived from headquarters and again she did not respond.

"One day, I can remember the sunlight through the windows upstairs in the salon falling through net curtains, making starry patterns on the floor. We heard then a loud knocking, a rapping on the door. My grandmother told me to get under the bed in the smaller bedroom. She said, 'Whatever you do, do not say a word. Do not breathe loudly. And never tell them where the dolls are hidden.' Then she hugged me and sent me under the bed where there was a dip in the floor and she pulled the rug over me as I lay in the dip.

"I heard more loud rapping. And then it seemed as if they were going to knock the door down and so my grandmother answered the door.

"Alas, the men came in. I saw their boots. They asked to see the dolls. My grandmother told them the dolls had been stolen a while ago. 'They are gone,' she said. She didn't know who took them. They trouped around the apartment. They continued to question and push my grandmother.

" 'No,' she said. 'The dolls are not here. I do not have them anymore.'

" 'Search the apartment,' shouted the officer.

"And so they did. They opened every cupboard, every closet, every armoire, and they dumped out all the contents everywhere. There were clothes and sheets and pillows strewn all around. They peered under my bed but because of the rug and the dip in the floor they did not see me. They turned over chairs and they knocked down bookshelves. I lay under the rug, under the bed alone and afraid. I knew where the dolls were, but I did not speak. I did as my grandmother told me."

Collette stops now. She coughs as if she is choking. Then she begins to cry. She cries and cries and we stand on the corner of the rue Michel-Ange and I do not know what to do.

Finally I put my arm around her and we sort of slowly limp along back to the apartment. We go into Collette's kitchen and she is still crying. I take her hand and hold it.

We sit down at the table. She takes a big, deep breath. "Yes, oh yes, they wanted those dolls. 'Very well, then,' they shouted, 'If you do not tell us where the dolls are, you will have to come with us.' And they took my little grandmother away. She was not going to betray France. She was not going to relent. Not this time. And she did not. I never saw my grandmother again." Collette sobs. And I cry too for Delphine Rouette and for Collette, who must have been so frightened lying under the bed.

"I should have said something!" Collette shouts. "I should have called out. I knew where the dolls were! 'Take the dolls but leave my grandmother here!' I should have said. But I did not. I obeyed my grandmother. I did not speak! I should have! I should have!"

"Collette," I say, getting up to hug her, "it's not your fault. It's not your fault. You were a child."

Collette cries and cries. "I will never forgive myself," she says. "They were only dolls. They were not worth my grandmother's life!"

"Oh no. You must forgive yourself. You are not to blame for a war. You are not to blame for the Nazis. You were obeying your grandmother," I say.

Collette and I sit together in silence then. A long deep quietness like a large body of water settles in around us.

"Where were the dolls hidden, Collette?" I finally say.

"Don't you know? Didn't you guess?" she whispers. "In your armoire! The seventeen dolls were hidden in your armoire. There is a false wall at the back of it that opens up and there are large shelves hidden in there. The dolls were tucked behind that wall, locked away in the secret part of the armoire in your room."

"Oh, Collette," I say and we cry again. We cry for Delphine Rouette. We cry for Collette and for all the children caught in the war. We cry for the dolls and for Madame Jumeau and Sylvie the spy and we cry for France and for what happened.

"There will always be tears in France because of that war," says Collette. "Those tears will never go away. We live with those tears. We work around those tears. But they are always there."

"Collette," I say, "what happened to the dolls?"

Collette looks at me. Her face is raggedy and red and she seems drained, as if all the light has fallen away from her now. She takes my hand. She gets up and we walk to the back of her apartment. There she opens a door into a small room.

Then I see them. Seventeen beautiful dolls, shining in their fancy bébé dresses with their beautiful handmade child bonnets with ribbons of smooth silk tied under their chins. There they stand on the shelf, seventeen perfect childlike dolls, untouched, unspoiled, representing France when she was thriving, when she was at her best.

Chapter 38

For the next few days a deeper quietness looms over the rue Michel-Ange, Michael-Angelo Street. The air is hushed and hot, the weeping wisteria shadowy and still. There seem to be no cars or scooters rushing by, as if even Michael the angel is standing too in silence with Collette. And then one evening the quietness seems to break.

I am sitting on the balcony in the late afternoon. How beautiful this city is and how complex, with its light and its dark side, its sparkle and its spell. I love to see the sun setting on the skyline here. I know it has cast its orange glow on thousands and thousands of evenings in Paris, even as Collette and Delphine tucked all those dolls in the back of the armoire.

I think about my armoire and how much it must have stored and kept in its life with its secret drawer and its hidden shelves. I remember when I first found the little doll dress with Jean-Claude. I remember the excitement and the worry as we opened the drawer.

And then I remember something else. Something I pushed aside and in my guilt almost forgot. There was some wrapping paper and a card with the dress. It had been a gift. I had shoved the ribbons and the rest to the back of the drawer. Maybe the card is something Collette would want to see.

The idea seems to stun me and then it sends me climbing back into the salon and rushing toward my room. In the hall I pass Dad, who is calling out, "Pet! Come and see the sunset. It's beautiful!"

"Saw it, Dad," I say, darting around him. I dash into my room and pull the chair away from the armoire. There is the little drawer with its bumblebee on the handle. I open it and gently lift out the wrapping paper and card.

I can hear Mom with Ava in the next room, saying, "Oh, honey, if I were your age I would wear ribbons in my hair. You should try it. That might look stunning."

"Collette?" I call out down the stairwell. "Collette? Where are you?" I scramble over the steps, slipping on them in my stocking feet. I tear across the foyer and stop at Collette's door. It's shut. It's locked. I pound on it. "Collette!" I call again. "I have something to show you!"

I run out the front door of our building and slip under another arch of wisteria and then I am in the courtyard in the back. The sunset is casting orange filtered light on the clothesline that stretches across the expanse. The large, sailing sheets are cast in a pale, orange glow. "Collette," I call again.

I see her standing among the sheets, the sky above her the color of a field of pumpkins ablaze with light. "There's something I forgot to show you! Collette!"

Collette looks out from the shadows and sheets and says, "*Qu'est-ce que tu dis?* What are you saying?"

"I have some wrapping paper and a card to show you. I forgot about it. It was all wrapped up, the doll dress. I opened it. It was a gift," I call.

"What did you say?" Collette calls back again. She drops her basket of clothes and clothespins and rushes toward me. For a moment it seems in my mind as if Michael the angel is lifting her up, carrying her across the courtyard toward me. She runs so fast she appears to be made of nothing but wind and clouds. "*Mon Dieu!*" she cries.

When she reaches me, I hand her the wrapping paper and ribbons and the card. She looks down at the card. Her hands are shaking. I wait. Moments pass. She throws her head back and looks up. She presses her fingers over her eyes. Her mouth trembles. I wait. She takes her hand away and looks farther and farther off, farther and farther up and away. I wait. Finally she drops her head down and reads aloud very quietly in French.

Then she translates it for me in an even softer voice. I almost cannot hear her.

Chère Collette,
You have just helped me hide the dolls. I want you to have this little dress and I want you to know that I am grateful for your help, my sweet child.
Love, from Grandma, 1943

"*Mon Dieu!* My skies! My trees! My water! My air! My life!" Collette cries out. "She was brave, my grandmother. She died with honor. She was courageous. She knew what would happen. She wanted to resist. And she thanked me. She thanked me."

Chapter 39

When I finally go upstairs it is nighttime. I walk in the darkened salon. And I sit alone in a Louis the Sixteenth chair. Paris is stretched out all across the front of the room through the long windows here, in the same way Collette's story seems to spread out before me. Every pore of my skin weeps for her and for Delphine.

At the same time Paris is showing me its other side, its dazzling nighttime colors. The lights and reflections sparkle like candles strung across the horizon. Moving spotlights span the darkness as Paris celebrates the night once again.

This apartment appears to be empty. When I pass Ava's room I see she has gone out. I try her door and find it locked again. Why does she lock it when she leaves? What is she hiding from me?

I walk through the rest of the apartment. No one has turned on any lights. Mom is sitting in the dining room with her back to me. Only Dad's study is lit up as he reads and writes astonishing things about some guy who died over a hundred years ago.

How sad I feel for everyone, sad for Collette and sad for Delphine beyond measure. I also feel terrible for Ava and Logan. And for what I did. Oh, I have to make that right.

I walk into the kitchen and see dirty dishes piled on the counter. All I can think to do in my sadness for Collette and for everyone is to clean the kitchen, the way Delphine made extra bloomers and dresses for free for Madame Jumeau to try to make up for what happened.

After I finish the dishes, I fill a bucket of soapy water and I get down on my hands and knees with a scrub brush and I scrub the white tile floor as if scrubbing away all the mistakes I've made. I guess I am trying to scrub away Collette's sorrow too. Hers is an old sorrow. I must scrub hard and long to wash that away. Finally the floor is clean and shines in that wet, fresh, renewed way.

Now I hear Ava returning. I hear her bustling through the apartment to her room. I hear her door closing. Now is a good time. I rush forward and knock on her door. "Ava?" I call. "Um, I have something I need to tell you."

"Pet, I don't want to hear what you have to say, okay? Leave me alone. I don't care what it is," says Ava.

I start to open her door. "Don't come in here!" she shouts. "Go away."

I just stand there with my head hanging down.

And then I too go to bed. I lie there staring at the ceiling. I never thought it would be so hard to take back something I did in one foolish moment.

I worry too about the fashion show. Every time I think about it, I feel like I am on a tightrope walking high over a flooding river. We shouldn't have sent in the application.

I am sure I will get rejected yet again. It's just another mistake.

Still, through all this, the feeling I have for Windel does not vanish, no matter how much I try to make it disappear. It hangs on like a line of music, a little phrase of melody that won't go away.

I remember coming across Windel in a Boston park in early spring. He was on the swings with his little seven-year-old brother, probably taking care of him for the afternoon. Both of them were swinging higher and higher. I watched them for a while from my hidden spot and then I realized they were both wearing headsets, listening to music as they were swinging. Windel took his off for a minute and I could hear it. He had been on the swing listening to Chopin's nocturnes. And his little brother was too.

After that, I went to the swing sets myself, even when it was cold out, and I would swing higher and higher, listening to Chopin. It got to be as if I became the music as I lifted up and down with the wind and the notes.

Chapter 40

Collette and I sit in the courtyard this afternoon. The plane trees blow and rustle their branches of hot green leaves, making a cleansing, healing sound. The sunlight and shadows flicker on the warm cobblestones. We drink some citron pressé, which is much like lemonade.

Soon Marguerite appears, carrying Albert in his cage. Marguerite loves Albert. "That bird has charmed everyone in Paris!" says Collette. "And you know Marguerite started with only a pair of finches in her cage at her apartment and now she has twenty-five finches. They make nests and raise families there! They produce the tiniest eggs!"

Marguerite smiles.

They begin to talk in sign language about Jean-Claude. Yes, he is always trying to kiss Marguerite. Collette translates the signs for me. "Yes, yes," says Collette. "He does that. He is very enthusiastic. Kissing and killing, you know, he is only doing what men have done since the beginning!" Everybody laughs. Laughter echoes against the four walls of the courtyard. "But he is a good boy, is he not?"

Soon we see Monsieur Le Bon Bon walking across the courtyard. He is coming back from his job. He walks toward us in a white jacket covered in white powder. Even his face and his small round glasses and his little mustache are all powdery white. He looks like a ghost from a Tintin book.

"Oh, Le Bon Bon, he works at the *boulangerie*. At the bakery. He is the flour sifter!" says Collette. "And he's back at work! *Enfin!* Finally."

"Oh," I say. "I didn't know."

Marguerite gives him a hug and a kiss on both cheeks, the French way to say hello. Soon she too is covered in white flour.

"This looks like love," Collette whispers to me.

When they are gone, the wind begins rinsing in the trees again. We sit quietly for a while listening to it. I look over at Collette to check her face. I find it has a fresh, clean look, like a floor recently scrubbed. "I rested well last night, my little angel, for the first time in a long time," she says.

"I am glad," I say.

"Sometimes it is good to speak, to say things, you know?" she says. "Hidden and unhappy things do not like the sunlight. It dries them out and they crumble away."

"I know," I say and I look down.

"Ah, what have you done about the letter and Logan?" says Collette.

"Nothing," I say. "And that's the bad part. I feel awful about what I did to my sister."

"Oh, my little one, of course you feel bad. Perhaps you can do something about it," says Collette.

"I have to tell her what I did but I haven't been able to find a way," I say. "She hasn't made it easy."

"Oh, *c'est dommage*! It is a pity," says Collette. "Perhaps you will have Ava as your model. You must make it up to her for what happened with Logan and the letter."

"What!" I say.

"Yes, remember the application said so. It said you must supply your own model," says Collette.

"I won't get in anyway. I'm sure of it. And Ava hates me," I say. "She locks her room when she goes out because of me."

"There are lots of things you have not talked about with Ava. And to lose a sister is a terrible thing."

"Oh," I say.

"Hmm," says Collette. And then she begins to hum a little song. I have never heard her hum or sing anything before.

"Well, shall we have some more citron pressé? Then I will go and lie down for a little nap," says Collette. "After all, I am eighty years old now."

"Collette! I thought you were only seventy-nine," I say.

"Oh, but I was yesterday. But today, not so anymore. I am now eighty."

"It's your birthday?" I say. "But you didn't get any presents."

Collette suddenly becomes very quiet and then she says in a kind of hush, "Yes, I did. I most certainly did, ribbons and all, my little angel. And I must thank you. It feels almost as if a spell has been broken, if you believe in such things." Then she hums the little tune again.

"Collette," I say, not understanding at all what she means about a spell being broken, "why did you say something about me needing a model?"

"Did I forget to tell you? Oh, *mon Dieu*!" says Collette, throwing her arms out as if to hug the sky in a French hello kind of way. "We received an email on my computer. This morning. We have heard from the panel at the fashion show! At last! You are one of ten finalists! Five of you will be selected to be in the show. And I am not surprised at all. What you did was absolutely wonderful. *Fantastique!* Naturally you are a finalist!"

"What!" I say. "It can't be. There must be a mistake. Are you sure?" The leaves seem to make a roaring sound in the wind now, like the ocean. Suddenly I drop to my feet and lie on the courtyard stones, flat on my back. *Me? Are you sure?* I stare up at the sky, the clouds racing across the blue. *Me? I am a finalist in the fashion show?* "Are you absolutely sure?"

"Of course I am sure," Collette says. And then she begins to hum her little tune again. And I realize she's humming "Happy Birthday."

Tears pour out of my eyes like rain blowing green across the courtyard. Streaming over my face. *They liked my dresses and my ideas?* "Collette, are you sure?"

She nods and keeps on singing. *"Joyeux Anniversaire. Joyeux Anniversaire."*

And then I join in with Collette. We sing "Happy Birthday" together, first in French and then in English, singing louder and louder and louder.

Chapter 41

After a while, I ride the tiny cage elevator upstairs. I truly feel like I am flying. *Me, a finalist in a fashion show? You mean, I have a chance? I could get in?* Moi? *Is that possible?* Yes, it's true because Collette showed me the email.

Nobody knows I applied, not even Mom and Dad. And I have a chance! Then a shadow drops over me. *Ava.* What about Logan's letter? For some moments I had forgotten. I don't deserve anything if I can't make *that* right. Oh, I feel terrible, awful, dreadful, and at the same time excited, amazed, and full of wonder. I am flying! The elevator stops and I step out singing and worrying at the same time. And I walk straight into Ava, who is all dressed up in one of her simple tailored sleeveless shifts, ready to go out.

"What are you so happy about?" says Ava. She's carrying a notebook. On the cover she has glued a picture of our dog, Lucy. Her hands grasp the notebook tightly.

"Oh, it's nothing, Ava," I say. "And where are you going?"

"Oh, nowhere," says Ava.

And then I remember Logan's letter again and I say, "Ava, I have something I *need* to talk to you about. Are you coming back soon?"

"Are you making a trip to the bakery now?" she says.

"I could be, I guess," I say. "I mean I wasn't, but yes, of course."

"A dozen cookies might be nice," she says. "And, um, a cheese sandwich with mustard. And maybe a bottle of sunscreen. Just leave it on the kitchen table for me."

"But I need to talk to you," I call out.

A pained look seems to cross Ava's face as she slips past me into the elevator and pulls the cage door shut. Then she waves through the mesh, reminding me for a moment of a terrible, beautiful caged bird.

In the apartment I pass Ava's door. It's locked again, as usual. But now I see Mom walk toward the door, unlock it with a little key, and go in. She leaves the door standing open as she makes Ava's bed with a lovely new yellow bedspread.

I stop in the doorway and Mom says, "Ava had a dream last night that her room was yellow and I wanted to surprise her with yellow curtains and a yellow bedspread. Want to help me, Pet?"

"Sure," I say. I take a corner of the light bedspread and we lift it high. It billows like a yellow flower opening above us and floats gently to the bed. The birds sing in the courtyard from an open window. Mom stands back, looks at the bedspread, and smiles.

"I'll get the yellow towels now. I'll be right back," says Mom. "Then Angus and I are going out to the Monoprix for groceries."

Suddenly I find myself alone in Ava's beautiful room after an entire month. Maybe I could write her a note about what I have done and leave it under her pillow.

I turn and go toward her desk looking for a piece of paper when I happen to see her dark armoire door is open. It is the sister to my armoire. Ava's armoire stands tall and towers too over her room. The door ajar, I see parts of dresses hanging in there. The colors from here look so familiar. Orange and maroon. I move forward and I look closer.

What I see throws me backward into the room. I land on the edge of Ava's bed, like an elevator that has just crashed to the basement, the wire snapping. All the pieces of what I see fly before me, like a flock of blackbirds leaving the courtyard below.

The wind turns and storms through the open windows now. The curtains blow into the room like ghosts set free. Everything racks and rattles with wind. The bedspread lifts and ripples. *What? No! No!* The dresses hanging in there stun me and seem to blow out all the lights in all the rooms in all of Paris.

Chapter 42

"No!" I shout, rushing past Mom with a pile of yellow towels in her arms. I tear down the stairs. I run out under the wisteria, out onto the rue Michel-Ange. It's afternoon, the air thick, and I feel almost as if I am struggling through hot, churning, murky water. Vines climb and tangle against many of the buildings. They seem to rustle in the dusty wind as if caught in a dream. The air presses and heightens as if a storm is coming.

I run down the street, not knowing why. *"No!"* I call out again. I rush toward the Laundromat, remembering the lost backpack. For some reason I stop there, looking through the window. I watch the wall of dryers spinning. The stolen letters and the stolen dresses tumble through the air in my mind, as if caught in a dryer forever.

Just then Collette comes out of the Laundromat with a wicker basket full of wet clothes. When she sees me, her face becomes a net of shadows. French gray clouds sweep overhead in the heat.

"Collette!" I call out.

"Oh, my little angel," Collette says. "You know I like to dry my clothes on the line, but we may get a storm now. And something has come up." I hear thunder rolling.

She looks away down the street. An empty cardboard box knocks along the sidewalk in the wind.

"Something?" I say.

"Yes," Collette says. She sighs. "We have received another email about the fashion show."

"No," I say again. I put my head on Collette's shoulder.

"I have pieced it together, *ma chérie*, and it's not good," she says. "Not at all."

Across the street we see Ava returning home. She doesn't notice us over here. She passes a lady with a dog on a leash. Ava kneels down in the wind with her knees on the sidewalk and pats the dog, rubbing its ears gently. Dust and leaves blow along the gutter.

Collette looks at me and her shadows turn darker. "The judges were confused by one of the entries. They had loved your designs and loved your essay about Madame Jumeau. They would have liked to award you a position, but they can't."

"Oh no," I say. "They can't?"

"No. Because someone else has submitted the same designs, *ma chérie*. The same dresses. That someone's essay did not mention Jumeau and that person was not a finalist. But now they are concerned," says Collette, looking down.

"Concerned?" I say.

"It brings up questions of originality, they said. They wondered, is there some kind of a mix-up, perhaps? Both parties having the same last name." Collette looks at me with sadness.

"Ava," I say.

"They offer any apologies, if the confusion is on their part. But as it stands, without an explanation, they wish you the best of luck in the future with your work."

"Best of luck? An explanation?" I say. And a terrible cape of disappointment closes over me. I press my head against Collette's shoulder and I start crying. "I saw the dresses in her armoire," I say. "She even used the same fabrics."

"Oh, *ma petite*," says Collette.

"Tell me it's not true," I say. And we watch Ava winding her way along the street all alone, staring down at the sidewalk.

Chapter 43

Now I storm into the salon. I find Ava sitting in a corner at a desk. Marie Antoinette in her garden is painted across its surface. Ava's long blond hair falls over the letter she is writing. I go stomping up to her.

"Ava!" I shout. "What did you do?"

Ava looks jolted and I see she's been crying.

"What did you do, Ava?" I shout again.

She looks up at me then and kind of recoils, as if I am shining a flashlight in her eyes. I glance down at the letter on her desk.

Dear Dad (if you deserve that name), Please do not…

After that, the ink is smeared. The paper looks wrinkled.

"What did you do to me, Ava?" I scream.

"What did you do to me, Pet?" Ava screams back.

"Ava, you copied my dresses. You sent my designs into the fashion show. You said they were yours."

"Oh, please," says Ava. "I copied an old doll dress. History does not belong to *you* alone!"

"But I found the doll dress. It was my idea to use it as an inspiration," I shout.

"I found the dress too. I used it as an inspiration too," says Ava.

"No, Ava, you used *my* dress as inspiration. You stole my idea."

"Ideas come from everywhere. They are in the air. You don't own the air. And what makes you so sure anyway?" says Ava.

"Because I applied to the fashion show too," I say.

Ava stands up. "What! *You* applied? How could you do that to me! You knew I was applying!!! You weren't supposed to apply. You're too young. I wouldn't have sent in those designs if I knew you were sending them in too," Ava shouts.

"That's not the point, Ava. You copied me. You took them from me. That's stealing, Ava. They know. They figured it out when we both applied."

"*Why* did you apply?" screams Ava. "Why did you do it without telling me? Now I'm embarrassed. You are always embarrassing me. I could just die." Ava throws her arms around herself and tucks her head down against her shoulder.

"Embarrassed?" I cry out. "You stole from me. How could you steal like that?"

"You stole from *me*!" shouts Ava. "You stole something precious from me."

"You mean the letter?" I say, trembling. My knees collapse. The floor buckles. I fall inside; everything seems to crash around me.

"Yes!" screams Ava. "The letter!"

"Ava, I only kept it for a few days! I was about to give it to you, only someone stole it from me before I could. I wasn't going to keep it. And I felt terrible about it. I tried to tell you, but—"

"But you *didn't* tell me," shouts Ava.

"I wanted to tell you, but I lost the letter. I didn't know how. I was trying to find a way. I was really sorry about that. But then when I found out what—"

"It was a ruinous thing you did to me!" screams Ava.

"It was a ruinous thing you did to *me*!" I scream back. "You copied my work! There is nothing meaner in this world! And you were copying me *before* I stole the letter! And it's not fair. It's wrong!!! And now you have to explain. We have to tell the judges. I would have been accepted! I almost made it in, Ava!!! You have to explain. They want an explanation. *I* want an explanation."

"No, I can't!" screams Ava. "And I won't." She grabs the letter to her father lying on the desk.

"Ava, you have to," I say.

"No, I don't!" she screams. "No. No. No." And then she drops down into a chair with her head against the back of it.

"Ava!" I shout. "You have to tell them what happened. You have to come forward."

"No!" she shouts. "I won't. It's your word against mine. Maybe *you* copied *me*!"

"Do I have to tell them what you did?" I scream. "Because I will! Collette knows! She gave me the other doll dress. She'll back me up."

"No!" Ava starts sobbing. "Don't do that to me. I can't. I can't come forward. I won't. I am sorry I did it."

"You have to tell them," I scream.

"I am so sorry. I wasn't thinking. Look how sorry. See how sorry. This sorry," she cries and she reaches in the desk drawer and pulls out a pair of scissors. With a quick motion, she chops off a chunk of long blond hair. It falls on the rug in a big shank.

"Ava, what you are doing?" I shout. But she keeps on going. She cuts another bunch of long, silky hair. Another and another and another, until her beautiful hair is chopped off, all uneven. Her mascara has blackened in rivers of tears all over her cheeks.

"What are you doing, Ava? Stop!" I scream.

"I won't come forward," Ava cries. "No. No. *No.* You don't understand. I can't. *You* have all the talent. I don't have any talent. I *can't* think of anything original. I can't do it. It doesn't happen for me. It happens for you all the time." Ava sobs. Her face looks twisted and smeared and she's all scrunched up against the chair. "It's not fair. You got all the talent. It was such a great idea. How did you do it?" She still has the letter to her father in her hand, and she crunches it up and throws it across the room. She slumps over.

How awkward she suddenly looks hunched over in the chair. Her feet seem large and sad looking. Does Ava have large feet? I never noticed before. They look puffy and swollen and miserable waiting on the floor below her. And I look at my perfect beautiful older sister all twisted up before me with her hair chopped off and her feet in those shiny wedge sandals.

I stand there speechless and stunned. My head spins and I can't hear any sound suddenly. Nothing makes any sense. "Ava," I scream. "What have you done to your hair?"

And then something terrible and strange sweeps over me. It comes in great shudders through my whole body. Something raw and new and painful pours through me. It comes with a kind of deep, wrenching, horrible blush. *Pity*. It is pity. Pity drops over me in waves.

Ava is sobbing and crying. "I shouldn't have done it but I had to. Dad didn't like the patterns I was using and you weren't going to show them, so I just thought . . ."

"But, Ava, you didn't need to do that. You have so much," I say.

"No I don't," she cries.

"Yes you do. You're so beautiful," I say. "Everyone says so."

"Who cares about that? Anybody can have that. Beauty fades," she cries. "It disappears. Look at Mom."

"Oh, Ava, you're clever. Look how great at math you are. I can barely add and subtract."

"But the dresses you make—they're good. How do you do it?" She has slipped to the floor now. She looks up at me kind of like a child. Kind of lost like that.

"What?" I say. "You *like* my dresses? I thought you hated my dresses. You're always making fun of them. I can't believe you like them," I say, starting to cry.

"I make fun of them because they are so beautiful. I mean, you come up with these things I could never do. I don't do anything like that. All I have is a father who I hate. An awful father. And he looks like me. Exactly, and he's horrible."

"How do you know he's horrible?" I ask. "You've never met him. I mean, not for years."

"I know because Mom tells me. She says he's horrible," says Ava. "And I feel horrible."

I look at her and am overwhelmed. I am on new ground. Fresh new ground. "But, Ava, you have to make up your own mind. You used to love him when you were little. Before Mom decided you should stop seeing him. He's part of you. You can't listen to Mom. She had her own relationship with him. It has nothing to do with you. I think not seeing him is messing you up. Collette thinks so too."

Ava rolls herself into a ball now. Blond Rapunzel curled up among shanks of her chopped-off hair, long swatches of it all around her. My perfect older sister.

"I am so ashamed, Pet. You won't tell Mom and Dad what I did, will you? Or Logan? I would die. Dad would be so disappointed in me. It would break Mom's heart. I couldn't bear it. I can't tell the judges what I did. I can't."

I close my eyes. I feel shattered. Bombed. And I stand there in silence. I don't know what to say or do. I am without words. I fall backward into a chair. I put my head in my hands. I can hear Ava crying. I can hear the traffic on the rue Michel-Ange.

Finally I whisper, "You won't tell Mom and Dad that I stole your letter? I would die about that. That was wrong too. It was terrible. I wish I had never done that but I can't take it back. I won't tell them about the dresses if you won't tell them about the letter."

"I won't, Pet. I won't," says Ava.

"Ava, what will Dad and Mom say about your hair?"

"Oh, I don't know. I don't care. I don't know where I fit in here and *you* have managed to break through. You have made real French friends."

"I have?" I say. I look at her and open my eyes wider.

"Yes, Pet, you're part of Paris now. And I am not," says Ava.

"But they would love you if they knew you," I say. "Oh, Ava, I didn't know how you felt. I didn't know." And I slide down on the floor next to her and I lean my head against hers. And then I take a deep breath and say, "You know what I think? I think you should see your other father. You used to miss him when you were five. Remember?"

Ava looks away quickly now and starts shaking a little. I can feel her shoulders trembling. "Ava, I think you should see him, if only for a couple of hours. I mean, Dad is your true dad, of course, but you should see him. Don't listen to Mom. She just wants you to be on her side. So you'll have two dads. Everyone will love you just the same. I will and Dad will and Mom will. Two dads will just be double trouble, in a good way, I mean. Collette says you need to discover who he is. He *wants* to know you."

Ava pulls back and looks at me. Her face that was shattered a few moments ago now looks quietly and oddly grateful. Her shoulders keep shaking, though, like the time she had a high fever and chills and Mom asked me to sponge off her forehead. She shook and shook and shook no matter how many covers we put over her.

"I mean, I'll go with you. He can be my second dad too. Two is always better than one. We'll call him Papa like the French do," I say.

Ava laughs at that and tilts her crumpled head. Then she looks down at her hands and she starts to cry again softly and so do I.

Soon we hear bells chiming and a dove cooing in rhythm with it, as if it is singing with the bells. And somehow Ava hears that and she stops crying and leans her head against mine and closes her eyes.

"Ava," I say finally. "For an explanation, I'll tell the judges that you are going to be the model for the clothes and that's why you sent the application in. You sent all that in as the model, thinking you were supposed to. We have to supply a model. Ava, I was hoping you would want to model the clothes. I mean, for the show. I mean, for me. I mean, after I explain, if they decide to accept us."

"Us? You want *me* to model your clothes?" she says.

"Yes," I say.

"What? Why me?" she calls out. "I stole from you. I betrayed you."

"It's okay, Ava. It's okay. I love you. I love you so much. We've been together our whole lives. Everything we know, we know together. Sisters are forever. *We're* forever. And besides, you will make a beautiful model. Even with your hair all chopped off, you are still beautiful."

"You want *me* to model for *your program*?" she says again.

"Yes, Ava," I say.

"Oh, Pet! I am so ashamed. I have been so terrible to you," says Ava and she starts crying again.

"Maybe we have been terrible to each other," I say. "But about the dresses, I forgive you."

"I forgive you too for stealing Logan's letter," she says.

"You do?" I say and I squeeze my eyes even tighter to keep back more tears. But they break through anyway.

And then something really amazing happens, something unusual, something really unexpected. Ava leans toward me and throws her arms around me and hugs me. "Oh, Pet," she says. "I will never forget this. Never. Never. Never."

"Ava, I love you," I say. "I love you and everyone there is gonna love you."

"Pet," says Ava again, "as Mom always says, you're the living limit. And I mean in a great way."

And then I say, "Ava, about the letter. I am *really* sorry I did that." And I reach for the scissors lying on the floor next to me and I cut off one of my braids and then I go for the other. They both fall away, long dark braids, and lie among the silky blond strands that once were Ava's crowning glory. We sit among lengths of brown and blond hair on the floor all around us. "There," I say. "It's only fair. I deserve that."

Ava shakes her shorn head at me. "Pet," she says, crying. "Look at us now. Just look at us." We both stand up and look into the mirror above the French mantle. Ava and I, side by side, staring at ourselves.

"You know what?" says Ava. "We look like sisters."

"Yup," I say. "We do."

I touch my hair. It's chopped off just below my ears. I have never had short hair before. My head feels lighter. I shake it. I feel different, springy, flippy, perky.

"By the way," I say as we both put on vanilla-flavored lip balm and try out different expressions in the glass in our new haircuts, "how did you know I stole Logan's letter?"

In the mirror Ava looks at me with her serious fern-green eyes. But there's a sparkle in them now, a flicker that dances across the surface, a light wavering in the distance in each of them, a light that is growing brighter and brighter.

"How did you know?" I say again.

Ava smiles and turns around and goes to her room and opens her drawer. I follow her. She fishes around in the bottom and pulls out *my backpack*. She holds it up by its straps. She dangles its squashed body in the air. My backpack! I fall forward now in amazement. My head starts to swim and I feel confused and mixed up and find myself wandering through a series of events, everything tumbling at me.

"Ava!!!" I shout suddenly. "It was *you* who stole my backpack and the letter! You stole it when I went to the Laundromat and left you at the café! And you didn't tell me! You let me worry and feel terrible all this time. And I felt so bad that I waited on you hand and foot! I did everything you asked! Everything. You outfoxed me, Ava!!" I shout. I can see in the mirror that I am starting to pout.

"Well," says Ava, "the letter was mine so I couldn't exactly *steal* it, could I? I didn't tell you because I knew you would torture yourself much more than I ever could. And besides, you *deserved* it! You tried to keep me and Logan apart!"

"But it didn't work?" I say.

"No," Ava says.

And then suddenly her words sink in and I feel a huge rush of relief. It pours over me in another great wash. "You mean, I didn't ruin everything between you and Logan?"

"No," says Ava. "He likes me! He likes me *a lot!*"

"Oh, Ava!" I say. And I throw my arms around her again. "I am soooo glad."

"And," says Ava, "I got a great sparkly silver sweater out of the deal."

"And tons of breakfasts in bed," I say. "And all your laundry done and everything else."

"And great sandwiches bought *and* delivered," says Ava.

"Ava, you outfoxed me!" I say again.

"Older sisters always outfox younger sisters," says Ava, beaming at me. "That is just the way it is."

"Ava, may I quote you on that?" I say and suddenly we both start laughing. Our laughter bursts and bubbles and coughs and I buckle forward again. We laugh and laugh and laugh. I feel as if we are laughing our way up to the ceiling and out the window, the Beanly sisters roaring away with the sparrows and the doves cooing, laughing with the bells of Paris ringing, laughing so much and so hard, Ava and I practically laugh our way down the Champs-Élysées and up to the tippy top of the Arc de Triomphe. And there you might see us, my sister and me, two short-haired girls, balancing, billowing, just laughing away in pure, total relief.

Chapter 44

Days roll by like piano notes in Paris or like the sound of the French language rolling out of everyone's mouth, mysterious music. I am sitting at the piano in the corner of the salon, my hands on the keys. I try to stretch my hands the full length of eight notes, an octave, but I can't reach. Like Delphine, my hands are quite small, which is good for sewing. Perhaps having large hands like Windel makes playing the piano the way he does possible. I feel a sadness but still a wonder at Windel's ability.

Just then I hear Collette in the hallway with Mom. "You know, I need a painting of Albert for Le Bon Bon as a going-away gift. You have this gift in America?"

"Uh-huh, we do," says my mother. "But who is going away?"

"Well, it has not yet been decided," says Collette. "But I think it is nice to have a painting of Albert. It will make Le Bon Bon happy! And I will pay you a hundred euros."

"Oh, well, that I may not be able to refuse," says Mom.

"And of course, many people who live on the rue Michel-Ange will see this painting and if it is nice they too will want one. Most of the people who live on the rue Michel-Ange have birds. Madame Turpin has already told me she might like a painting of Aimé, her little cockatoo," says Collette.

"Oh," says Mom.

"And so while you are here you might have a little business, as you put it in your country, and make a few bucks, *n'est-ce pas?*" Collette says.

"Oh," says Mom. "Well, I will be very pleased to paint Monsieur Le Bon Bon's bird."

"You can use a photograph and then of course I can bring him upstairs in his cage. He'll love the attention!" says Collette.

"I do have a canvas. Is it a large space? It might be the perfect size to fill that gap on Monsieur's wall. My husband bought me the canvas a while ago. That's a coincidence, isn't it?" says Mom.

"Perhaps," says Collette.

Then their voices fade as they go downstairs to look at the space. I play a few notes on the piano with one finger. Then I add a few more, making a kind of little tune that seems to describe for me the sadness I feel about Windel, the relief and forgiveness I feel about Ava, and also the gratefulness I feel for Collette and her friendship.

Chapter 45

Dad was away for a couple of days and returned yesterday. Now he comes bustling into the apartment at the end of a rainy afternoon. "Okay, so it finally happened just as she predicted," Dad says. "I was caught out in the world without Grandma Beanly's umbrella!" He stands there reminding me of a soaking-wet American rabbit in a dripping beret with a loaf of soggy French bread in his paw.

Ava has been napping but she's up now, wandering around with her jagged hair sticking out in places. Yesterday we wore hats to hide our cut hair from Dad. But not today.

Dad stops in his tracks looking at Ava and says, "Ava! What happened to your beautiful long hair? Where is it?"

"It's in the garbage," says Ava. "I cut it."

"Me too, Dad," I say, standing next to her.

Dad's eyes go wide and he steps back a few paces and looks at us for quite a while. "Ahhh, I shall forever be mystified by you two, just as we are mystified by the moon and the stars in the sky," he says.

"Yada yada, Dad," says Ava.

"Well, actually, girls, I have got a surprise for you too. Buddy, come here," he says.

"What, Angus?" Mom calls from the dining room. "Are you upset about the girls' hair? I know you wanted us all to live in another era, but the truth is, Angus, we don't. And you come in here. I'm too busy to get up," says Mom.

"Too busy for *me,*" says Dad, looking slightly bruised. Dad goes into the dining room and Ava and I follow. "Buddy, wow! You're painting. That's beautiful! It looks just like Albert. And I love the colors."

"Well, did you expect anything less?" says Mom.

"No, Buddy, I didn't," says Dad, putting his hand on her shoulder.

"Look, can you guys go in the other room now? Angus, you're disturbing me," says Mom, looking at her painting and then down at her palette of colors.

"What?" says Dad.

Then Ava and I kind of drag Dad into the hall. "Look, girls," he says, pulling up his sleeve. "I got a tattoo. That's my surprise!"

"Oh no," Mom calls. "You're not the type, honey. You have to be a motorcycle man to have a tattoo."

"Not a Flaubert man?" Dad says.

"No," says Mom and she gets up and quietly shuts the dining room door.

"What?" calls Dad. "Now we match. We'll be twins with tattoos, Buddy. You won't be embarrassed about your tattoo 'cause I've got one too."

"What's it say, Dad?" I ask.

"You see the book? Well, on the book it says *Je lis les romans de Flaubert,* which means 'I read the novels of Flaubert.' "

"Oh, Dad, that's dorky," says Ava.

"Ava, there is nothing wrong with a bit of dork now and then. To be dork-free is to be boring!" Dad says.

"You're cute, Dad, so we forgive you," says Ava, and she kisses him on one cheek and I kiss him on the other. He has a daughter on both sides of him, as usual, and he's smiling.

And then I look over at Ava with caution. I nod my head at her. She nods back. So I say in a quiet, careful voice, "Dad, um, Ava is thinking about seeing her other dad. Actually, I mean, just to say hi and, you know."

"Really, Pumpkin? When did this happen?" says Dad. He kind of puts his hand on the back of a chair to steady himself.

"Oh, yesterday, I guess. Sort of. When he called again in the afternoon, I answered the phone. We talked a little. He told me he and his family are staying in the town of Versailles," says Ava. "I might go out there for a short visit. Well, he's going to drive in and pick me up, actually. Pet might come along."

"Well, that's a good idea, Pumpkin. Girls," says Dad. "A really grand and fine idea." Then he gets quiet for a minute. And he puts his arm around Ava. "And don't worry about Buddy. I'll walk her through it. I know all this has been hard for you."

Ava closes her eyes. "Thanks, Dad," she says.

"We'll just be going for a quick chat. No big deal," I say.

"Ava, you will always be my Pumpkin, you know that," Dad says.

"I know that, Dad," says Ava.

"But," says Dad, changing into his joking voice, "don't stay more than an afternoon. No longer. Okay? Promise me?"

"Okay, Dad," says Ava.

"And are you girls ready to go to Flaubert's house this weekend? Buddy, what do you say?" he calls out to Mom.

"Dad, we've tried twice. We never make it there. Something always stops us, like the protest—and then the last time that water main broke in front of our car and flooded the engine and the front seat," I say.

"Yeah, I know. Perhaps I wasn't meant to go there. I Googled Flaubert's house and as I suspected, there's no house there anyway. It's just the garden and a small pavilion left. The house was torn down and the whole place is surrounded by smoking factories. It would break Flaubert's heart to see it. He wanted life to stay old-fashioned and handmade. And he was right!" Dad calls out.

Then a deep sadness comes like a shadow over Dad's face and he just stands there with his arms wrapped tightly around Ava and me.

Chapter 46

Yes, the days roll by in Paris, like a French song sung on a small side street in a trilling voice with an accordion playing. Yes, the days roll by and, of all things, Ava and I have plans to go to a movie this evening. We haven't been to a movie together since I was eight. Ava had eaten something spoiled earlier and halfway into the movie she threw up on my lap. I am hopeful things will go better this time. We're planning to see an American movie with Brad Pitt so we figure it will be in English.

Dad says, "Hey, what's the flick? Can I go along?"

"A flick? What's that?" says Ava.

"Angus," says Mom, "don't horn in. Let the girls do something alone for a change."

Personally I like to get dressed up when I go to the movies. I like to get dressed up whenever I go *anywhere.* So I put on my green cotton sundress and hat I made especially for this trip to Paris. Ava doesn't say anything when I walk into the hallway. But she smiles. I feel pretty happy with the green color and the fall of the skirt and the choice of fabric. *The judges liked my designs. Ava likes my designs.*

Recently I have been feeling pretty good about stepping out on the streets of Paris. I see all kinds of wonderful and different and weird clothes. Some long and lacy, some short and puffy. Summer hats of all sizes and shapes and colors. Silk scarves flowing or knotted or worn around the waist.

Collette helped me write an email to the panel at the fashion show explaining the mix-up, as they called it. We told them that Ava was going to be the model and had sent in the dresses she was going to be wearing. They were so cheered, they wrote back, to clear up the confusion. And so pleased, they said, to include my designs in the show. I admit to crying a little when I read that.

Ava and I ride the tiny elevator together now and when we pass Collette's closed door we find a woman sitting in the hallway where Collette often sits. She seems to be pleasantly waiting for Collette.

We go out under the wisteria and hit the sidewalk. The Beanly sisters in Paris. We walk by a van parked right in front of our building, with gold French words on the side that say *Musée de la Poupée de Paris.*

I look around for Collette but I don't see her out here watering the flowers with her green tin watering can, as she often does. There was something about that kindly woman sitting there in the hallway. Something that gives me a pinch of unease.

Musée is museum, I am thinking. *Poupée* means doll. So the van says "Doll Museum of Paris." Oh. I take a deep breath. I feel quiet all the way to the soles of my feet. I wonder what Collette is doing. Why is the museum van there? Who was that patient-looking woman?

We get to the end of the street and turn. I notice immediately the lamppost on the corner has a flyer wrapped around it. Being the curious type, I take a look. Ava noses over and sees it too. We're on the Avenue Mozart now. I haven't had the greatest of luck in this area so far.

"Look," says Ava, "it's a flyer about your shoe. And look, wow, they have glued a photo of your shoe on the flyer. And it says something about one shoe being found and it says if anybody knows the owner of the shoe, they should contact the manager at the Hôtel Magique. You should go over there and get your shoe."

"Oh, I can't," I say. "No way. There's someone staying there I don't want to run into."

Then we arrive at the movie theater. We buy a bunch of candy. Unfortunately we get into the theater, find two cool seats in a perfect location, and then we realize Brad Pitt is saying things like *"Bonjour, mon vieux,"* and *"Mais non!"* We sit there, mostly clueless, munching chocolate.

As we polish off bar number three, Ava whispers, "So are they going to have rehearsals for the fashion show? I mean, so I know what to do. I mean, I can walk the walk, I've practiced it a zillion times since I was twelve, but you know, are they going to rehearse?"

"Well, I don't know if *they* are, but we're going to, aren't we?" I say.

"Well, yeah," says Ava, "definitely." Ava hands me another chocolate bar but I can't manage it. My stomach is turning in circles. I'm feeling upset about that shoe flyer. I mean, I hate to abandon my personal property but I am not going over there and risking running into Windel Watson again or his mother, for that matter. The last time I went near the Hôtel Magique it was a total disaster.

Now on the screen there's a cowboy scene with Brad Pitt on a rearing horse and people shooting each other. Jean-Claude would love this part. There's smoke and noise and in the chaos a horse in the background appears to get shot and slides into the dust for atmosphere.

That's when we stand up to leave. If a horse gets shot, Ava always leaves. It doesn't matter if the horse is in the background, just part of the scenery, and probably didn't really get hurt at all. That's where Ava draws the line.

We walk back down the Avenue Mozart. I suggest turning a corner to get slightly farther away from the little side street that houses that dreadful hotel. We seem to pass several more of those shoe flyers pasted on streetlamps.

"Honey, look! Here's another flyer! You've got to do something about it!" Ava says. It's been years since Ava has called me "honey." I am happy to hear that word, even though it has a slight ring of superiority about it. But it's a superiority younger sisters are used to and expect. It's a *dependable* superiority, one we can count on in this world of chaos.

"Honey," she says again, "you have to go get that shoe. It was a great shoe!"

"Great?" I say. "You liked the shoes?"

"Well, I mean, they were a little weird, but cute in a way. I mean, with that mouse on the toe. It's worth going back for the one. What good is the other shoe at home? You can't wear one shoe."

"No way," I say again. "I am not going anywhere near the Hôtel Magique. And I am not going to explain why, so don't ask."

I also don't correct Ava about my shoe and the mouse on the toe. I don't tell her she's wrong and that it is a poodle. I just let it pass. Older sisters do not like to be wrong. They enjoy being right. They are happier and nicer when they are right. Even when they are dead wrong.

Chapter 47

Oh, I have so much to do to prepare for the fashion show. I have taken out the hem on each of the four dresses and lengthened them. And because Ava has a thin frame, they now fit her beautifully. It was astonishing to see Ava wearing one of *my* creations, especially the maroon-and-orange one inspired by Delphine Rouette's doll dress. Suddenly Ava was part of everything that has happened to me in Paris. She was part of the cinders and the sparkle. The light and the dark. The happy and the sad things.

Ava and I have started rehearsing together. She has been practicing changing outfits as fast as she can behind a makeshift screen. Mom has been timing her. I have decided on the order in which each dress will be presented and I have written my little introduction talk. I have also chosen the music with some help from Dad. He and Ava have chosen this really old song "Oh! You Beautiful Doll."

Yesterday I went over to the embassy and met everyone, and no one could believe (until they met me) that I was only twelve. Mom went with me. On the way home she said, "Didn't Ava send in something to the fashion show?"

"Yes, she did," I said. "She sent in my designs because she was going to be modeling them."

"What happened to *her* dresses?" Mom asked.

"She didn't send those in because she used bought patterns," I said. "We decided this was better."

Mom looks over at me, kind of wounded and kind of pleased at the same time. "Oh, I get it," she says, smiling. "That sounds lovely, honey."

Then we stopped and bought some thin lavender cotton fabric for the dress I will sew for myself to wear that night.

I haven't seen much of Collette lately and that makes me feel anxious. Today outside her door I see a little old-fashioned suitcase with a leather handle sitting there in the hall and no sign of Collette, but then I run into her on the street and feel better.

"Oh, my little angel," she says, hugging me. "I love your new haircut. You look so *à la mode*!"

"Well, Dad liked our old-fashioned long hair. But he'll get used to it," I say.

"Oh, I can't wait to see your fashion show. I will be there early. I am so pleased. Are you going to sew yourself a dress to wear? Would you like to use my sewing machine? I can bring it upstairs for you."

"Um, actually Ava says I can borrow hers," I say.

"Well, isn't that wonderful, my angel. I am so happy to hear that. And did you see Le Bon Bon and Marguerite? They are becoming good friends! I guess my work is finished here. Almost," she adds, looking at me with a little bit of worry.

"What do you mean your work is finished here?" I say.

"Well, things are settling down, in a good way. A concierge always likes to see everyone in her building smiling," she says.

"Oh," I say. "Of course."

"And what is this flyer I keep seeing with a picture of your shoe on it?" she says. "You must go over to the Hôtel Magique and fetch it."

"Never mind about that," I say. "I don't need that old shoe. And I do not want to run into Windel Watson and his mother."

"Ah, Windel Watson."

"He hates me and so does his mother," I say, trying not to look miserable.

"Well, you must go to the Stewarts' for dinner. Is it tomorrow night? Going out will be nice, *n'est-ce pas*?" says Collette.

"Maybe," I say.

"Well, I must go now. I am pleased with the painting your mama did for Le Bon Bon. Madame Turpin is coming over to see it. And she is bringing Madame Poulin, who has a small pet turtle. Do you think your mama can paint a turtle, making it look just a tiny bit better than it really is? That turtle of hers is no beauty."

"Oh, I am sure she can," I say. "Well, I am off to get some purple thread for my dress. Good-bye, Collette!"

"Oh, don't say good-bye, my little angel. We never say good-bye in France. We say *au revoir.* Do you know what that means? It means 'see you again!' "

"See you again, Collette."

"*Au revoir,* my little angel."

Chapter 48

I am not sure where I can buy lilac-colored thread. I mean, they don't seem to have any Ben Franklin stores around here. I go to the end of the rue Michel-Ange and look down the wide boulevard. Vehicles of all sizes, especially tiny three-wheeled trucks, go whooshing by.

Maybe it's the wind on the wide boulevard, making me feel tossed and tussled and solitary, but I see Ginger in my mind again. She's standing in silence. No smile. No frown. On the table near her sits a crystal ball, of course. She doesn't pick it up this time. It's snowing inside the ball. Snow is spinning all around in there in whirls and eddies. Funny because this is Paris in July.

Before the terrible basement incident, I can still remember the day it snowed in April. I had been listening to Windel playing the piano, sitting outside his door at the practice building. I think he was playing something called "The Seasons" because I remember peeking in the little window on his door and seeing the cover of the music on the piano before he started. The Seasons. Spring. Summer. Autumn. Winter. All described and etched in sound as Windel's hands flowed over the keys.

Afterward I followed him outside into a surprise spring snowstorm. It was wet, heavy snow that stuck to everything. Trees and branches and leaves bent low with the weight. Windel stepped right out into the middle of the empty street and stood there, letting the falling snow gather all over him. I was hiding behind a tree but I had Ginger's camera with me and I leaned out and got a photo of Windel from the back, standing in the snow with his arms outstretched, as if flying. It was a great shot. A rare shot of Windel alone. I actually still have the photo, even though it's all wrinkled and torn.

And then it hits me.

I walk through the little park near our street with renewed awareness. Oh, moon and stars that change and move forward with our Milky Way! Oh, universe that Dad says is expanding and moving forward constantly! Everything changes and quivers and yet some things won't budge. Like a crush that won't quit. Try as I might to change things, I will always be in love with Windel Watson.

And then I walk past a puppet show. Little French children are sitting before a painted puppet stage and laughing at a sad puppet clown, who is hopelessly in love with a beautiful ballerina puppet. The poor clown tries to win her heart, but he keeps getting knocked down over and over again by a suave prince with a big blue hammer. The sad clown must spend his life making others laugh while he gets pounded on the head. I definitely feel a kinship.

Chapter 49

Yes, Ava accepted an invitation for the whole family to have dinner at the Stewarts' apartment. But how did Collette know that?

Mom evened out my hair and Ava's hair yesterday. She used a brand-new shiny pair of scissors. And last night she put Ava's hair in curlers. Ava is so excited about the dinner. She was in the bathtub for hours this morning and Mom is now taking the curlers out of her short hair in the dining room. The pink spongy curlers drop away to the floor and Ava sits there with a white sheet over her shoulders, looking so much the same and so very different.

It's a hot summer evening. Dad and Mom and Ava and I walk a few blocks, headed for the Stewarts' apartment building on the avenue Ingres. We pass a park. There is a merry-go-round there all lit up in the dark and a fenced-in ring next to it where a pony draped in flowers with a braided mane waits with his trainer for children who might want to have a ride.

And when we bustle into the Stewarts' building, some big puppy dragging a leash comes clumping down the stairs and rushes toward us. My luck, another dog.

"Oh, come back here, you little rascal," calls Mr. Stewart, lumbering behind him. "Catch that leash, will you?" The puppy drags the leash between our legs. But of course it gets tangled around mine and I slip and almost twist my ankle. Then the fluffy puffball starts barking at me. He nips at the edge of my skirt and tugs on it, pulling on me. "Grab that leash, will ya?" calls Mr. Stewart again.

Dad leaps in and snatches the leash finally and we rein in Logan's big puppy. But alas, I arrive at the dinner party somewhat shaken, with wet puppy teeth marks across my skirt. I suddenly get a quick flash before my eyes of Ginger again and a crystal ball that is rolling away from her. It's rolling down a hill and Ginger is chasing it.

The apartment is lit up with candles and all the windows are open and all of summery hot Paris lies below us, stretching far and wide, like an enormous paper flower covered in lights. I find myself on the threshold of the Stewarts' salon ahead of everyone.

"Oh, hello, Pet! Lovely to see you! Cute haircut! So happy about the show coming up," says Mrs. Stewart, greeting me French style, a kiss on each cheek, and just when you think it's all done here comes an odd third kiss for extra measure, leaving it all unbalanced and confusing. Just like everything in France.

"Ava, dear, you look splendid. I love your hair! Did you two get cuts at Demander La Lune?" says Mrs. Stewart.

"They do such a good job there. It's just around the corner from your place."

"Not exactly," says Ava, smiling at me.

"Well, come in, everybody!" says Mrs. Stewart. "My dear friend Nan just called and said they are running a little late so let's just relax and have some hors d'oeuvres, shall we?"

"Nan? Nan Watson?" I say out loud, feeling like I got on that merry-go-round downstairs and it just broke off its track and is spinning off into the universe. *How do you stop this thing? Screech!* My eyes span the room, tumbling across the furniture, stumbling over all the faces.

"The Watsons?" I say. But nobody hears me. My knees start trembling. There are lots of Watsons in the world. Hundreds of them. Thousands of them. Why do the very ones I don't want to see have to be coming here tonight? And I thought it was just going to be a cozy dinner with the two families. I didn't know the Watsons would be included. Why didn't I stay home?

Everybody is patting Logan's puppy, who just came back in with Mr. Stewart. "We went to get him in Rouen. He's going to be huge. He's a baby Russian wolfhound," says Logan, putting his arm calmly and surely around my older sister. I feel a swooning in my heart for Logan and Ava.

"Russian wolfhounds make wonderful pets," says Mrs. Stewart.

"They're especially wonderful in the middle of the night when they need to be walked," says Mr. Stewart.

"Logan wants to be a veterinarian, Dad," says Ava. "He just decided. What do you think?"

"Terrific," says Dad. "Then I can go see him for free if anybody ever steps on my tail."

"Dad," says Ava. "That is sooo lame."

"Ava," I say in a low voice. "*The* Watsons?"

She gives me a worried look.

I now make a quick dash toward the salon. I need a place to hide. Under a table possibly? No, the baby Russian wolfhound would surely find me and start barking.

Since I don't see any caves or deep crevices around here, I sink down into the long-lost, lovable family couch. Oh, I have missed this American icon! A real couch! One to curl up on with a warm bag of fries and a cheeseburger in hand and a TV clicker and nowhere to go but down into its deep, fat, soft cushions.

I look quickly around me and my eyes land on a big coffee-table book. I grab the book and pull it up toward my face. It is called *The Paintings of Henri Matisse.* The guy obviously did a lot of work in his lifetime. This book weighs a ton. Yes, Matisse the French painter, one of Dad's buddies. Collette likes him as well. Now he is fast becoming *my* favorite too. I pull a small blanket over the rest of me and prop the book up close, squarely in front of my face.

Soon enough I peer over the top of the book and see the piano in the corner. A piano plus *the* Watsons equals *Help!* What am I going to do? Mrs. Watson will be here. I mean, Nan. No! I don't want her to report me to my principal. I want to continue my life somehow, like a normal girl, having sent in my schoolwork from here and hoping to move on into the eighth grade like everybody else this fall.

Alas, moments later, I hear the front door open, followed by the usual hustle and bustle of arrival. The kisses and the gifts and the excitement. It's always the nicest moment of an evening.

Soon everyone pours into the salon and I begin studying up close one of Matisse's paintings, really close. The one called *The Red Studio.*

Logan pats Windel on the back. I hear the friendly thump of it and then Logan says, "So, Windel, you made it over the big pond. What, did you bring your piano with you on the plane? I bet that caused some major turbulence."

"Yeah, no, I actually left it at home. It was pretty heavy and wouldn't fit in the plastic tubs at the X-ray machines," says Windel.

Ava laughs. Logan introduces her to Windel. The words he uses have a luster and a glow. They sparkle. "This is my *girlfriend,* Ava," Logan says softly. And those words drift in the air like confetti.

Then Mrs. Stewart says, "So, Windel, how do you like Paris?"

"Well, whatever you're feeling, Paris will double it. If you are happy, Paris will make you ecstatic. If you're sad, Paris will make you sadder," Windel says quietly.

How true, I am thinking. My knees are still shaking. I look closer at the painting of Matisse's red studio. It's the reddest red I've ever seen. It's a burning, beautiful, heartfelt red. I will float into the red studio and hover there forever.

"It's a good thing Windel is happy," says his mother. "Because when he's sad, his music gets morose and dark. Doesn't it, Fritz?"

"Yeah, but he *is* sad, Mom," says Fritz, the little brother. "He wouldn't go out yesterday for any reason. He just moped around the hotel all day."

"Speaking of music," says Mrs. Stewart. "Honey," she says to Mr. Stewart, "you know the CD I play all the time? My husband thinks I have lost my marbles but I listen to it constantly. This is the boy who wrote it. He wrote the song. Play some piano for us, Windel, will you? Maybe some of us will dance? Like say, perhaps, Logan and Ava?" I hear Logan and Ava murmuring and then the light notes of laughter. "Sing the song for that girl. Erin? You know the song you call 'Small Surprise'?"

"Okay, sure," says Windel. He takes a kind of tall, baggy, corduroy bow and he goes to the piano. I peer over the top of the Matisse book. Oh, I know that stance, the way he leans forward and then throws his head back before he puts his hands on the keys. He always looks up before he starts, like there's a smiley face on the ceiling above him.

First he plays a short Chopin piece. Oh, I know this piece so well. So many times when he was practicing and I was crouching outside his door, he would start with that. How beautifully the music flows from his hands tonight, as if suddenly all of Paris has been fused and sealed into the notes, the rolls and the rises and the rain and the rushing of wind. I'm breathless and overwhelmed. Secret tears spill all over Matisse's red studio.

When the piece is over, Mrs. Stewart calls out, "Windel, you are a wonder. Isn't he? And just thirteen years old! Please sing the song you wrote called 'Small Surprise,' the one for that girl. You told me her name is Erin, right?" she says, whispering to Logan.

Logan whispers back, "Shhh. Yes, Mom. Erin Barslow."

"Well, you'll have to forgive my singing voice," Windel says, pushing up his long, grandfather's sleeves and smiling again at the ceiling. Then Fritz comes over and sits with him at the piano and Windel puts his arm around him for one moment. And then he begins:

You're a dragonfly.
You light up my eyes.

You're a butterfly.
You're my small surprise.

The tall French windows along the wall are open and the lace curtains blow into the room like ribbons set free and all of Paris seems to pour in and swirl and billow through the room, wrapping itself around us, making everything flutter and move.

You're a dragonfly.
You light up my eyes.
You're a butterfly.
You're my small surprise.

Now Logan gets up and draws Ava out into the middle of the room and gently, easily they start dancing. She bends with him and he bends with her. They are close and tight and when I peek over the edge of the book, Logan's face is lost in a kind of freckled, dreamy trance. His red hair is tumbled against Ava's curly, cropped hair.

You're a dragonfly.
You light up my eyes.
You're a butterfly.
You're my small surprise...

Behind Matisse's book, my heart turns and twists and breaks and breaks and breaks. Ava and Logan. Windel and Erin. I push my nose against Matisse's easel in the middle of the red studio. I lean my cheeks against the red studio chair. My forehead is lying on the red painted ceiling. Erin Barslow must be the luckiest, luckiest, luckiest girl in the world.

Suddenly the song is over and Ava and Logan come toward me. They flop down next to me, one on each side, and I get my breath back and I choke out a whisper to Ava. "Help! Get me out of here," I say.

"Okay, honey," says Ava. "Done." I look over the book and see all the parents lined up near the piano. They form a kind of wall around Windel.

Then Ava whispers to Logan and he reaches around me and picks me up in his arms. For once I am glad to be small. I pull the blanket up over my head and I lie covered like a dead body as Logan carries me across the room.

At the doorway Ava calls out, "Mrs. Stewart! My sister has a headache. Logan and I will take her home. We will be back in a flash, it's only a few blocks away."

"Oh, honey, what a shame," I hear Mom calling. "You'll be missing dinner. We'll bring you something, okay?"

Fritz comes up to us. I hear the patter of his little feet on the parquet floor. He leans over me and says, "What happened and who is *that*?"

And Ava says, "Oh, it's nobody. We'll be back in a few minutes."

Nobody. Nobody at all.

Unfortunately we pass Windel's mother in the hall and she boldly lifts the blanket from my face and peers down at me. "Oh! Is she okay?" she says but her face seems to glare in a wordless, silent way, as if to say . . . *Not* you *again! If you want to make it through school, steer clear . . . Stay away . . .*

Logan sweeps me forward and we hurry off. I push my face against his shoulder, thinking that Logan is fast becoming one of the best big brothers anybody ever had.

In the rush of feet and doors shutting I hear other things too. Windel saying, "Will she be okay? Who was that?"

"It's Ava's sister, Windel. She just has a headache. It's nobody you know," says his mother.

Nobody. Nobody you know. Nobody at all.

Now I'm in a complete desolate blur. Embarassed, humiliated, rejected. The three mainstays of a true bumbler. I hear more pieces and parts of conversation. Everything seems broken and mixed up, like sentences tumbling in a dryer. I hear Mrs. Stewart say, "Windel, that was wonderful!! WWW-dot-fantastic! Thank you for playing that. When is your performance in Paris? And who is this Erin Barslow?"

And just as we are closing the door, I hear Windel's voice saying, "My performance is next week." I hear two chords playing. Then a single note. "And um, I don't really know Erin. So, yeah, no. The song's not hers."

Chapter 50

I am sitting here in the hall this morning, staring at the landline telephone. How do you call the States anyway? How many numbers do I have to add and where does the zero go? Is Ginger asleep now or would she just be getting up? Or is it midafternoon back home in America? I am all mixed up.

My hand hovers over the telephone with caution. The only time it ever rings is when someone wants to reach the Barbours, like people who call themselves friends and don't even know the Barbours are in America. I pull my hand back.

I heard from Ava last night that the party thinned out to mostly adults and wasn't that great. When Logan and Ava got back to the party, Windel was gone. His mother and brother were there, though, and Mrs. Stewart left Windel's plate in place, hoping he'd come back but he never did. I didn't plan on the Stewarts' party turning out badly. If I had known Windel was going to be there, I never would have gone. Honestly, Mrs. Watson. Nan. I do not wish to stalk your son anymore and it was completely by accident that I even went to that party.

But I don't have time to dwell on it. I have to keep working on the show. It's coming up at the end of the week and I have so much to do to get ready. I just have to work around all this. Even though the song called "Small Surprise" seems to play in my head constantly, running like a sad, sweet undercurrent behind everything, like the river Seine moving through Paris and never stopping no matter what happens.

Two days later I am just ironing the hem of a dress. The hot steam rushes up against my face with the whoosh of the iron as it glides across the skirt. I hear the apartment door open and Ava blusters into the hall. I poke my head out and see she has a pile of mail in her arms. "The strike must be over. Dad! You got some mail!" she says, dumping letters and packages all over the floor.

"Did I get anything?" I ask.

"Yeah," says Ava. "You got so many letters from Ginger that she's probably the reason the post office people went on strike."

"Hah! Good old Ginger," I say, laughing and gathering up all her letters. It will probably take me forever to read them all. But I start with the last one, the most recent. I take it with me on a walk downstairs and outside. It's a warm rainy morning as I step out along the rue Michel-Ange. I open the letter and drops of water fall across Ginger's crazy handwriting.

Hey Pet,

You never write me!!! I don't know what's going on in Paris. Veronica Brown wants me to help her with her crush on Peter Bartin. So I have been busy!!! And Melanie Tanly wants help too with Stevie M. so things are pretty crazy here. I am flooded with phone calls. I now have a sign over my office door that says "Ginger's Crush Management Service." Do you like the name?

And oh! I just wanted you to know I found your awesome pink jacket!!!!!!!! You know, the one you lost on Valentine's Day. Oh my gosh, you must have left it in my laundry room (my office now) after we got home, because I found it behind the dryer yesterday. It was kind of wrinkled and rumpled so I was going to wash it for you. I checked the pockets and guess what I found? A sealed envelope addressed to you in the pocket. I opened it, Pet. Hope you don't mind. It was a valentine!!!!!!!!!!!! You got a valentine from somebody!!!! It was unsigned. Still, I thought you would be pleased. I mean, who gets a valentine these days? I mean, Veronica Brown told me she didn't get one. Neither did Melanie Tanly. Hope to hear from you soon, Pet.

More later,
Ginger

A little bit of rain splashes across my face as I walk along the street. A sprinkle of wonderment, a dash of sparkle. I got a valentine from somebody. Even if it was six months ago, *somebody* gave me a valentine.

The valentine seems to follow me around in a nice kind of way. As if wherever I go there is a little bird flying behind me just out of sight. But there's still so much to do to get ready for the fashion show!

As the week wears on, Friday night looms closer and closer, like the moon getting bigger and fuller and more yellow. Friday night soon. Soon. *Somebody gave me a valentine.*

Ava and I are so nervous that we have done nothing but rehearse. We haven't left the apartment for any reason. Ava has popped in and out of that dressing screen so many times it's uncountable, and she is now so fast she has become an almost invisible blur in between dresses. And I have memorized and gone over my short talk so many times that when I am an old lady and dying I will surely spout the whole thing as my last words.

Dad keeps coming into the salon and saying, "Girls, I have planned a trip to the Victor Hugo Museum this afternoon. Did you know he was a painter as well as a writer? Come on. Let's get geared up. I think the place will surprise you."

"Um, no thanks, Dad," we say in unison. "We're busy."

I have also finished my lavender dress. It has a waist and delicate tucks all across the front, inspired, as the others, by Ernestine Jumeau's doll dresses. It has twelve small mother-of-pearl buttons down the back and tiny buttonholes that I sewed while trying to watch French TV with Ava. I thought of Delphine Rouette and her lost sister while I stitched the buttonholes. I was glad Ava was sitting next to me, going through the antique button box Collette had loaned me. Collette told me the word *jumeau* means "twin" in French. In a way, Delphine Rouette was almost my twin. Almost.

When I was at the embassy they told me I could show five dresses, that I could add one more to the collection. And I have been working on that one. It will be the finale, the last dress on the runway since I will be the last presenter.

Now we are very close to Friday night and the fashion show and the full moon. The moon now reminds me of a big yellow crystal ball in the dark sky getting bigger and closer every evening. And when it's Friday night and time to go, it almost feels like we are stepping right into that crystal ball. The yellow glowing lights of Paris bloom around us as we drive in a car rented for the night.

"I didn't want to get stuck in the metro with all your dresses and hangers or trust some French cabdriver who might go shooting off into the Fifteenth and circle around on the Périphérique for hours. Better this way," says Dad, driving past churches and parks and fountains and people sitting in outdoor cafés under strings of lanterns.

Ava has gone long and cold and pale curled against her backseat window. I feel the same way. Bubbles of stage fright gurgle through me. They call it *le trac* in French. I have *le trac. J'ai le trac. Ava a le trac. Nous avons le trac.*

When we get to the Place de la Concorde, all the domes of the buildings seem to be dipped in gold. All the statues too. Dad lets Mom and me and Ava off right at the marble steps to the entrance. This isn't the embassy. This is some other building made of carvings and cut stone. I see a French flag and an American flag billowing from poles as we go in.

We pass two large columns that mark the entrance to the ballroom where the fashion show is being hosted. Ava and I get name tags and then we look out at the large crowd sitting in many, many rows of chairs. Ribbons frame the long yellow velvet runway. Logan gets up and waves to us. He stands out in a crowd with his red hair. He holds up a folding chair almost over his head, letting Mom know he has a place for her and Dad. *Somebody gave me a valentine.*

Ava looks greenish-gray now and as if she might throw up. My hands too are shaking slightly. "Ava," I whisper. "We practiced this so much. We know what we're doing."

And I kind of lead my older sister (a first) to the backstage area. As I draw her along, I feel a kind of inside strength, something sure and unflappable and new.

There are four other designers here and all of them have made beautiful clothes. We can hear the announcer now beginning the program.

"Welcome to *Sew! You're in Paris*," he says and he thanks a list of people and goes on to talk about the show. Then he announces the first student designer, Dana Trumbell. Dana comes up and tells the audience the clothes she has designed were meant to capture the essence of a garden party in South Carolina, where she is from. The dresses are all in chiffon pastels. Next, a student from New York City goes to the microphone. He tells the audience that his designs are in black and white exclusively.

I miss seeing the other two presentations because I am helping Ava hang up and organize our dresses. And when I hear my name announced, I sort of freeze. Then I fumble and bumble out onto the stage area and stand before the microphone. I feel dizzy and as if I might faint, and then I look out at the audience and I see Collette sitting there smiling at me. She nods gently. She is sitting with Jean-Claude and Monsieur Le Bon Bon and Marguerite. My friends. My true friends. Ava is right. Nobody in my family made friends with France like I did. Not Mom. Not Dad. Not Ava. *Me.* I made friends with France. And somehow even before I begin speaking, I feel another rush of sureness.

I lean toward the microphone and say, "*Bonsoir*, Collette and everyone. *Bonsoir.* Good evening. When I first came to Paris, I found a doll dress in my armoire. And I wanted to know more about it. This dress sent me on a journey to discover and appreciate the doll clothing created by Madame Ernestine Jumeau of the Jumeau doll company here in Paris. In her day, Ernestine Jumeau was as important and famous as a designer as Coco Chanel. Everyone waited to see her new designs for doll dresses every season in the 1880s and 90s. After all, these dolls and doll dresses were shipped all over the globe, sometimes to remote places. In this way, everyone in the world could see the latest Paris fashions. My collection of dresses has been inspired by Madame Ernestine Jumeau and one of her best couturier seamstresses, Delphine Rouette.

"First we will see these four dresses and then I will speak to you about the last one. Please welcome my sister, Ava Beanly, who will be modeling the line."

Then the music comes on. *"Oh, you beautiful doll, you great big beautiful doll."* Out comes Ava in the orange-and-maroon silk-and-velvet dress. She walks to the end of the runway and then back again. She turns, poses, and turns again. Then she dips into the back room and reappears rapidly in the next dress. *"Oh, you beautiful doll. You great big beautiful doll."* She does all four dresses without a flaw.

When the song ends and Ava is changing, I go back to the microphone and say, "This next dress will be the last. I designed it especially for Delphine Rouette and for her bravery and courage and sacrifice during World War II."

No music yet. Just silence. Ava walks out and stands on the runway with her eyes closed. She is wearing a black sailor dress with a long yellow silk tie at the collar that trails almost to the ground. The black collar has two yellow stars appliquéd on each corner at the back. She stands still and the music begins:

Oh, ma patrie, ne pleurez pas,
ne pleurez pas, vous et moi.
Nous allons guérir, comme la lumiére,
comme le ciel, comme le vent,
comme la terre.
Oh, ma patrie, ne pleurez pas,
Ne pleurez pas, vous et moi.

Oh, my country, do not cry.
We will heal, you and I.
Like the light, like the earth,
like the wind, like the sky.
Oh, my country, do not cry.
We will heal, you and I.

Ava in the black drop-waisted sailor dress stands tall and straight as the music ends. But then something amazing happens. The entire room full of people begins to sing aloud together.

Oh, my country, do not cry.
We will heal, you and I.
Like the light, like the earth,
like the wind, like the sky.
Oh, my country, do not cry.
We will heal, you and I.

The whole room is ringing with the song as Ava stands alone on the runway. Until the song is finished, the stage lights dim, the houselights go up, and the show is over.

The audience cheers and thunders and stamps their feet and cries out. They shout, "*Vive la France! Bravo! Chapeau!*" Some of them shout, "Hats off! Hats off to you!"

Then people are swarming around Ava and me. I talk with a man from the École de l'Art. And Logan comes up and hugs Ava and kisses her right in front of everyone. People start telling me how much they loved my dresses and the program.

And finally Mom makes her way through the crowd. She throws her arms around me and holds me tight. "Oh, Pet, it was wonderful! Beautiful. And I love you so much."

"Thank you, Mom," I say. "I love you too."

"Pet," says Mom, "about your dresses—I just didn't understand until now. I'm so sorry, honey."

"Mom," I say. "Mom, it's okay."

"And you and Ava were a true sister team. I loved seeing you two together like that. That's the way it should be," says Mom, hugging me again.

"Mom," I say, "some guy told me they want me to go to their art and design school on the Avenue Mozart. He offered me some kind of scholarship. They only speak French there."

"Oh, well, you'll learn quickly," says Mom. "You're young."

"I hope so, because I want to go there," I say. "I think."

"Of course you do, honey. I am so proud of you," says Mom.

Then Dad comes rushing up and grabs me and Ava and says, "Girls, you were great! You wowed us! You blew us away!" Then we kind of form a four-way hug, Mom and me and Dad and Ava, all in a big circle, embracing. And I am thinking, we came to this crazy country and we felt like lonely outsiders and somehow we just don't feel that way anymore.

Chapter 51

Now the crowd is moving quickly. Everyone is milling here and there. People keep stopping me and telling me they loved the show and why. And I keep saying thank you. But all I want to do is find Collette. Where is she? And then I see her squeezing through the crowds coming toward me.

"Oh, my angel. Thank you so much for that tribute to my grandmother," she says, hugging me. "Oh, nothing could have meant more to me than to have everyone singing that song. It was as if they were singing for her and for me." Collette has tears in her eyes as she holds both my hands together in her hands.

"Collette, I've missed you," I say. "Where have you been?"

"Oh, dear. I guess you saw the truck from the doll museum," she says.

"Yes, I did see it. I wondered about it," I say.

"Well, I finally called them because I wanted to give the doll collection to them," Collette says. "After all, everyone should be able to see those dolls and enjoy them, not just you and me."

"What did they say?" I ask.

"Well, they told me because it is a complete set they are very valuable so it seems, and they insisted that they give me at least a portion of the money. I finally had to accept. I got tired of saying no. And it will be a help. I can live in my little *maisonette* in Provence now, the little cottage that belonged to my papa. I have always wanted to grow lavender."

"You're going there to live?" I say. "But who will be the concierge for us?"

"Did you meet Elise?" she says.

"You mean the lady who was sitting in the hall that day?" I say.

"Yes, she will take the job. You will like her. And I am now free to go, and you helped me with that. Oh, my little angel, you have released me. After all, I am eighty years old. I have lived in that apartment all my life. I do not need to live and dwell on the past anymore."

"But you can't leave. You're my best friend," I say.

"We will always be friends, Petunia. No matter where I am," she says.

"But you're like my fairy godmother. I mean, I know it sounds stupid," I say.

"Oh, but I am only a concierge," says Collette. "And it's sad because concierges are going out of style in Paris. They have a reputation for being nosy. But that is not right at all. Perhaps a concierge *is* kind of like a fairy godmother in a way, each one looking after all the people who live in her building."

"But if you go away, I'll miss you," I say, starting to cry.

"I will miss you too. When I see my field of lavender flowers stretching far and wide, I will think of you and your lavender dress, my little angel. But I must go now, sooner than you would believe. Did you see the other van parked in front of the building last week?"

"Yes I did. I wondered about that too," I say in a very somber voice.

"Ah. It was a moving van, *ma chérie*, and it is all packed now. I didn't want to tell you until after your show. And you were so busy upstairs preparing your program that I was able to pack quietly without any fuss. I wanted you and Ava to do your very best this evening, and you did! But the movers are planning to drive the van tonight. You must understand, they like to drive when it is quiet, no other cars on the road. I will sleep in the backseat. We will leave at midnight. The air will be cooler and better for travel."

"Oh, Collette, I wondered what you meant about a going-away present. You knew you were going away! Oh, and thank you for your help, Collette. I mean, with the French seams and your sewing machine and Ava and everything."

"Well, we helped each other, *n'est-ce pas*? Isn't that what friendship is all about? Now, for you the night is young, my little angel, and there's more to come. Try to enjoy it. After all, you earned it." Collette hugs me and I hug her and I don't want to let her go. But she turns and waves and then walks into the crowd of people. When I see her moving through the packed room toward the door, she seems suddenly frail and I want to rush over and hug her one more time. But I turn my head for a second and when I look back, she is gone.

Chapter 52

Now I stand in the midst of the crowd. For a moment I feel a great aloneness. I spin around and I start to unravel, my old unsureness returning. Then someone comes up to me and pats me on the back. It's Ava. "Here you go, Pet," she says, handing me a purple bouquet. "To match your dress."

"Oh, Ava, flowers!" I say. "They are beautiful! This is the third bouquet I have gotten this summer."

"Thank you. Thank you. Thank you, Pet," says Ava, giving me a hug.

"You too, Ava," I say. "You did such a beautiful job. Nobody could have done it better."

Ava smiles and looks away across the crowd. She points her long arm toward the other side of the room. "There are some very cool pastries and cakes over that way. You might want to get over to them before they are all gone," she says and then she too slips away.

I look across the ocean of room. The smell of wisteria and lavender and summer lilacs from the bouquet in my arms sweeps over me. My head is light. I feel faint. Way on the other side, almost against the wall, my eyes suddenly flutter and stop still and fall on Windel Watson floating like a boat on the surface of this ocean of room.

My head starts to swim. The cloudy wisteria and lavender in my arms makes me sway a little back and forth. Even from this great distance, Windel seems to find me with his serious dark eyes. *If you're sad, Paris will make you sadder.* Is he extremely angry or extremely sad? He's waving something above his head. It looks like a hammer. Does he know that it was me who ruined his performance and dinner at the Stewarts'? Me again?

"Oh no!" I murmur. "I better get out of here."

I drop to my knees and end up crawling away with my bouquet in the opposite direction from Windel through a jungle of feet and legs. Some of the people above me lean down as I crawl by and say, "What a wonderful group of dresses you created!"

"Thank you," I mumble from my hands and knees as I scramble forward. At the edge of the room, I slink back up to my feet and look around and I see Windel's face again. Everyone is a blur, a dab of color, a swatch of paint, everyone except Windel. He still seems to be frowning and waving something that looks like a shadowy hammer. "I need to get away," I whisper and I push and nudge and crawl until I get to the door.

I roll out into the night, dashing across the lit-up Place de la Concorde surrounded by its glittering domes of gold and the Grand Palace. I run farther and farther down the street until I get to the bridge called Pont Alexandre III. I rush halfway across it, passing cherubs with trumpets and horses with wings and the Seine river, golden and glowing in the nighttime lights.

Suddenly I get another image of Ginger. She holds up her hand to stop me. In my mind I see the little valentine floating, floating in the air. I stop in the very middle of the bridge and take a breath and turn around for a split second.

I see Windel Watson at the beginning of the bridge. He's starting to cross it. The wind rolls and rumples his shirt and his corduroy jacket flaps. He's calling out something.

"Petunia!" he shouts. "Wait! Stop. I have something to say. I didn't write that song for Erin. I wrote that song for *you*!"

"What?" I whisper.

"I liked you listening to my music. I liked you being there! In fact, I *loved it*!"

"What?" I say again.

"I loved it. *You changed my life!*" he shouts into the night air.

"What?" I say in disbelief. And then as Windel gets nearer, I focus clearly on him in the glowing darkness. I look closer at him and realize he isn't carrying a hammer at all, but a shoe, my missing shoe with the poodle on the toe.

"What?" I call out.

He comes forward in his red high-top sneakers, sweetly, gently, corduroy flapping, dark hair blowing. *Somebody gave me a valentine.*

"I could never have practiced so long or played so well if you hadn't been there listening to me. When you crouched by my practice door all those hours, it changed my music," Windel says.

"You *knew* I was listening to you?" I say. "You knew I was outside your door at the practice rooms?"

He pauses. Then he rolls his eyes toward me and looks over the tops of his glasses and says, "Yes. They had installed TV cameras a year ago for security in all the practice rooms so people at the pianos know who's coming to the door. They can see on a TV monitor."

"Oh no!" I say.

"But you were so adorable, like a little elf out there on the floor. You were listening so intently. You understood what I was doing. You were my first fan! *I* got better because of you!"

"You saw me? I was on your TV monitor?" I say again.

"Yes," he says, folding his hands into his grandpa's big baggy corduroy pockets.

"Oh no," I say. "I'm so embarrassed!"

"No, no," he says. "I saw you when you thought no one was looking . . . I saw the *real* you and I could watch you as much as I wanted. All the music I played, I played for *you*."

"What?" I say, and I begin to feel a little flutter, a pinch of something like unfolding wings inside me.

"Once I came across you in the park in Boston. You were swinging on my little brother's favorite swing and listening to music with a headset, just like I do. I was on a bicycle but managed to get a photo of you," he says. "I keep it with me. Look." He pulls from his jacket a wrinkled picture of me on the swings.

"It's kind of torn," I say.

"I know," he says. "But I carry it around a lot."

"You mean you were stalking me while I was stalking you?" I say, looking at the photograph, feeling breathless.

"Well, you could put it that way. But when two people are stalking each other, that's what you call *love*," says Windel. "Or double stalking. Same difference."

"Oh!" I say. And then I reach up to shoo away a beautiful yellow moth fluttering around us. And by mistake, I knock Windel's glasses off and they go flying over the edge of the bridge and drop into the Seine river. We both stand there peering over the railing as Windel's glasses float in the current, headed for the suburbs of Paris. "Oh no, I'm so sorry, Windel," I say.

"Your short hair is so pretty," he says, looking at me. "Really pretty. And don't worry about the glasses. They have clear lenses. I just wear them to look more serious. There's this guy from some band years ago and I didn't want to . . ."

"Well then," I say, "let them go."

"Remember Halloween? I mean, why do you think I took Fritz trick-or-treating on your street?" he says softly.

"Oh, Windel. I didn't realize. I didn't know," I say. "But I am glad I got to meet your grandpa that night."

"Thank you," says Windel, closing his eyes.

"And I am so sorry I lost your overcoat," I say.

"Hey," he says, "that was my fault. I forgot to bring my coat that night. We got a ride to the school and I didn't notice. I thought I'd left it at the coat check. When I got home my coat was on the couch."

"It was?" I say. "Then whose coat did we mail to you?"

"I don't know," says Windel, "but it was a *nice* coat and it fit me too."

"Oh," I say, suddenly worrying a little bit about Veronica Brown and Melanie Tanly, wishing them luck with Ginger's Crush Management Service.

Then Windel shakes his head and looks at me very sadly. "That night at the Stewarts', there I was singing the song I wrote for you and I didn't even know you were there behind that book. I figured it out after you had gone when Fritz called your mother Mrs. Beanly," says Windel, looking down. "Then I got really upset."

"Oh," I say, wondering if my knees are going to fold up under me and collapse. Windel leans back against the railing. Papers, sheets of written music, slip out of an inner pocket and scatter all across the bridge, flying away into the wind. Windel shrugs his shoulders and smiles at me.

"All those months you listened to me play, I didn't want to say anything. It was so special, I didn't want to break the spell," says Windel.

"The spell?" I say, feeling as if the little bird inside me is opening her wings now wider and wider.

"I hope you'll want to go to my concert next week. I *need* you there. I put a ticket for you inside your shoe."

"Oh, thank you, Windel," I say, taking my shoe.

"And by the way, that's one great little poodle sitting there on the toe," he says.

"You noticed! You knew it was a poodle!" I say. And the little bird inside me seems to spread her wings full span.

"What else would it be?" he says. And suddenly he wraps his extra-long, floppy, corduroy Windel arms all around me, and I fall against him. My head knocks into his iPhone in his shirt pocket and I hear a click.

"Oops, I think I just took a photo of the inside of your shirt pocket, Windel," I say.

"Hey, there aren't enough pictures of shirt pockets in this world. And yes," he says, looking down at me, "*you* are my small surprise. Because you shouted 'Surprise!' as you ran away from me."

And then he kisses me on the end of my nose. And the end of a nose is the perfect place to be kissed when you're on the middle of a bridge full of lights and cherubs and golden winged horses. And my heart begins to soar finally like the nightingale when it flew from the courtyard up, up, up into the sky.

Epilogue

Ginger's mom says bumblers are just people who haven't yet found a way to succeed at something. And perhaps she is right, because I didn't seem to bumble much else in my life after that night. Maybe I never bumbled anything in the first place. I just thought I did.

And it was all because of our trip to France and Dad's sabbatical. And no, a sabbatical is not a book bag, not a backpack, not a suitcase. No, as far as I am concerned, a sabbatical is just a great big gift given to the whole family, out of the blue.

That year I never got around to writing my book *How to Be a Younger Sister* and in fact I guess I don't have any clear-cut advice. It isn't always easy. Just hang in there. And if you do, the rewards are great. I mean, *who* changed the mixed-up course Windel and I were on? If Windel hadn't come to the fashion show that night, he would have soon gone back to America and he and I would never have found each other. So *who* invited him?

Well, if I had been a small child sitting outside a flower shop on the corner of the Avenue Mozart one afternoon, I might have seen a tall, short-haired blond girl wearing a dark raincoat and sunglasses, sneaking secretly over to the Hôtel Magique. I might have seen her dart into the lobby and then quickly leave an invitation on the desk for Windel, signed in her hand without anyone knowing . . . *Hope you can come to this. Can't wait to see you. Love, Petunia Beanly.*

Author's Note

When I was a young girl I lived with an American family on the rue Michel-Ange in Paris. I cannot begin to describe the magic and wonder I felt being in Paris then. All my life I have longed to stay once again in that apartment with the balconies on the rue Michel-Ange. And so it was a great joy to join the Beanlys in my imagination and to live there again with the piano in the salon and the red-haired concierge and the nightingale.

Later, as a grown-up, I stayed in Montmartre with a Frenchwoman and her daughter who raised finches in a lovely large cage in her kitchen. From the window at night there you could see the lit-up dome of the Sacre Coeur just across a courtyard. The Frenchwoman's name was Collette. Although my Collette is very different and much older than she was, still I was inspired and touched while I stayed there.

And finally, a few years ago my husband and I rented an apartment for four months in Paris. We lived just off the Avenue Mozart at the top of a little building on a side street. I could walk to the Auteuil Market that I remembered as a teenager and I could even linger on the rue Michel-Ange.

It is so mysterious how stories happen. Reality, memory, longing, and imagination all seem to sing together a little song and if you listen closely, sometimes you can get some of it down on paper.

Acknowledgments

Thank you so much to Rachel Griffiths, my talented editor, to whom this book is dedicated. As I am always saying, "What would I do without you, Rachel?" Special thanks also to the incomparable Arthur Levine. I just feel so much at home and so happy to be part of the family at Arthur A. Levine Books.

In fact, thank you to all my friends at Scholastic. How lucky I am to work with all of you! That is, Kelly Ashton, Sue Flynn, Jana Haussmann, Jazan Higgins, Ann Marie Wong, Lizette Serrano, Antonio Gonzalez, Bess Braswell, Tracy van Straaten and the publicity team, Mary Claire Cruz, and Elizabeth Krych. And thank you to the adorable and funny Nikki Mutch!

I also want to thank my readers, that is, my dear friend Sarah Wesson, Yvette Feig, and Bob Murray, and my sister Marcia Croll, who listened to the book over the phone as my beautiful mother once did! I am also grateful to my French friends Antoine Polgar and my truly charming and brilliant French teacher at Middlebury College, Mireille McWilliams. Georgette Garbes Putzel has also been a terrific French teacher. Thank you! Many thanks to Karen Kane, who helped me find my way in Paris. And to Ron Fisher, my brother-in-law, a fine French speaker. Thank you to François Theimer and Florence Theriault for their wonderful books on collecting and appreciating Jumeau dolls. And I am grateful for the doll shops in Paris and their owners, who were always willing to talk to me and answer all my questions.

I also want to thank writer and critic Leslie Fiedler and his wife, Margaret, for taking me to Paris to live for three months when I was a young girl. Thank you. I miss you!

And finally, thank you to my husband, David Carlson. The poem he wrote to me many years ago called "Dragonfly" inspired the lyrics to Windel's song "Small Surprise." Thank you for the poem and for your friendship and love, which have kept me afloat in all kinds of storms.

May I say to all of you: "Thank you! Love you! Where would I be without you?"

About the Author

Phoebe Stone is the beloved and acclaimed author of several middle-grade novels, including *The Romeo and Juliet Code*, which was hailed by the *Boston Globe* as "quite simply the best novel for young readers . . . since *Harry Potter and the Sorcerer's Stone*." She received four starred reviews for *The Boy on Cinnamon Street*, and another star for her novel *Deep Down Popular. Booklist* awarded a starred review to *Romeo Blue*, the follow-up to *The Romeo and Juliet Code*, calling it "compelling, and with plenty of heart and soul." Phoebe and her husband live in Middlebury, Vermont.